BEYOND THE SILENT PRAIRIE
A LOVE STORY

Sequel to PRAIRIE RATTLERS, LONG JOHNS
and CHOKECHERRY WINE

Emma L. Willey

PublishAmerica
Baltimore

First printing

ISBN: 1-4241-1310-5
PUBLISHED BY PUBLISHAMERICA, LLLP
www.publishamerica.com
Baltimore

Printed in the United States of America

Proudly, I dedicate this book to my husband, Orman O. Willey, my partner for more than 62 years. This is actually our love story. Our life together is continually filled with variety and fun. My helpmate and partner, he encourages me in everything I attempt. Readers will learn we had fun along the way with our work in many different fields. We moved around a lot, and proved what the author's father often said is true: "a rolling stone gathers no moss." What we gathered in our years together means more than gold — a lifetime of wonderful memories, and most of all, our loving family.

Orman and I both wish to dedicate this book to our descendants:

Children:

Valerie Faye Willey McGee and husband Terry
Alyce Marlene Willey Johnson and husband Norm
Orman Ray Willey and wife Katie

Grandchildren:

Jennie Lynn Stubbe Whitten and husband Al
Todd Marlyn Stubbe and Emma's mother Stacey
Eric Norman Johnson and wife Amy
Ryan Scott Johnson
Jesse Ray Willey
Kristamae Willey

Great-Grandchildren:

Emma Corrine Stubbe
Olivia Grace Whitten
Elliot Eric Johnson-Pritchett

We wish for all of you success in your lives, and the same kind of happiness and love we have known.

Table of Contents

~CHAPTER 1~
FINDING MY SOUL MATE

Sister Ruth and I graduated from Sorum High School in June of 1939. Ruth, our other sister May and I felt quite grown up. May had only one year of high school left, and by then our eight older brothers and sister Anna left home one by one to marry or start working away from home. The three of us realized we too would soon be leaving the prairie and Spring Creek Farm where we all grew up. The youngest three of twelve siblings, we needed to make some future life decisions.

My two sisters and I sat on the bed in our upstairs bedroom talking while we organized our clothes after getting home from high school — Ruth and I for the last time.

After some sobering thoughts, I said, "I wonder where we'll all be five years from now."

"I know one thing," Ruth said. "I'm going to get out of South Dakota and away from the family and find out what's out there in this world."

"Not me," said May. "I want to stay here and marry my boyfriend Cliff and be a rancher's wife in a few years."

I said, "I think I'll go to Chadron, Nebraska, to business college because I have a scholarship there. I'll learn to be a bookkeeper or accountant." I hadn't decided for sure yet, but I wanted a career before marriage, and I hadn't yet found anyone I wanted to spend the rest of my life with. I could tell Dad wanted me to date a young man from church.

9

"Do you really think Dad will let you go all the way to Nebraska?" May said as she folded up her last pair of anklets and put them in the dresser drawer. Ruth agreed my plan might not sit well with Dad.

"There's another thing," Ruth said as she hung up her prom dress. "I think it's about time we quit using baby talk and stop calling our parents Mama and Papa. All the older kids call them Mom and Dad, and I think we should too." May and I agreed, and from that day on we called our parents Mom and Dad and they didn't even seem to notice the difference. Our discussion ended when the wonderful aroma of roast beef wafted up from the kitchen. We went downstairs to see if we could help Mom with dinner.

One morning at the breakfast table Dad announced, "Ruth and Emma, I have decided I will send you to Black Hills Teachers College in Spearfish. You can go to school one year and earn a First Grade Certificate like your older sister Anna did. You'll qualify to teach in a country grade school here in Perkins County. May, you'll go with them and finish your last year of high school in Spearfish. We'll find an apartment for all of you to live in while you go to school."

What choice did I have? I didn't want to be a teacher, but Dad was paying the bills. I decided to be a teacher first and pursue my other dreams later.

Dad rented a small apartment in the back of a house in Spearfish, about halfway between the college and the high school. Ruth and I enrolled in college and May started her senior year in high school. We shared the apartment with Mary Seymour, a neighbor girl who lived just a few miles from us in the prairie country. Just like we did in high school, we packed groceries at home to take to our apartment. It was too far to go home every weekend like we did in high school, so we packed up lots of Mom's home-canned meat, fruit and vegetables.

College professors were tougher and getting straight A's

didn't come easy anymore. It had been fun to sing in Glee Club in our little high school, so I tried out for the soprano section; however, when the chosen names were announced, I didn't hear my name. It wasn't on the bulletin board either. I put the disappointment behind me, buried myself in the required subjects and began to prepare to be a teacher.

We spent most of our time doing homework and walking back and forth to school. Not having a car, we walked everywhere and attended any free entertainment in town. The Passion Play was held in Spearfish each year and was free to students. One Saturday Mary and I walked up on the side hill to sit on the grass and watch the play. Two boys from back home sat down beside us — my old boyfriend Bub from high school and his friend Orman, who had graduated from the Agriculture School in Brookings, South Dakota. When the play ended, they walked home with us. I didn't know it then but that day I began a relationship with the man who would eventually be my husband. I think I fell in love with Orman because of his fun-loving ways, so different from the serious life I was used to at home. I definitely wanted to see more of him, and we continued to see each other during the college term.

Ormie and I walked everywhere, and once he managed to scrape up enough money to take me to a movie. One weekend we took a long hike to the top of Lookout Mountain. Ruth met a student named Chet who owned a car and was the only student on campus who had one. One weekend Chet invited Ormie and me to go for a ride with them to Spearfish Canyon at the foot of the Black Hills. The winding road took us through the pine trees up the narrow canyon road until we came to a little lake nestled between two wooded hills. Ormie and Chet took Ruth and me out on the lake in a little rowboat, then for a hike up into the hills above the lake.

Ormie and I became good friends and got together whenever we could. He stayed in the basement of the

11

dormitory where he worked taking care of the boilers, working to pay for his tuition. I even visited him there a few times. I often helped him with his English lessons, and to this day he tells people I did his book reports for him. I don't think I actually did them for him, but we discussed them together because we took the same required classes since we were both preparing to teach school.

One night we rode in the back of a big truck with a bunch of other college students to go to a football game in Deadwood. It was a cold snowy night, so we dressed warm, and the excitement of the game and cuddling together on the stadium seats kept us warm.

We graduated in June and went home for the summer. Ormie and I both qualified to teach in a grade school now. He drove thirty miles from his parents' ranch to ours to see me several times that summer, but we had a problem. Dad didn't like my boyfriend Ormie; in fact, he really didn't like anyone who came to take his daughters away. I think he wanted to choose our mates for us, and preferred someone who attended our church. But I didn't love any of them.

One night when Ormie came to pick me up to go to a dance, Dad got in his car, drove down by the creek and stayed there until we left. That didn't sit well with either of us, so we came up with a plan. The next time he came to see me, I purposely stayed upstairs for a while to let Ormie talk with Dad. After Dad opened the door, Ormie stepped into the living room and spoke first, saying, "I think it's time you and I have a talk."

Dad asked, "What do you have to say to me?"

"I love Emma and I intend to ask her to marry me someday, but I would like your approval first," Ormie said.

"Thank you for asking me. I appreciate it," Dad answered. And he added, "I think you're okay." When I got downstairs, I could see they were on friendly terms.

Armed with my First Grade Certificate in the spring of 1940, I was hired to teach the Beck School, a little country school. I made arrangements to room and board with one of my patrons, Hiram and Mary Dutton. Their son Harold was one of my students whom I taught in the 7th and 8th grades. Their daughter Helen also started her first teaching job that year. I rode with her the short distance to my school and she continued on to hers farther east in the county. Dad drove me to school every Monday morning and came after me on Friday night. Once in a while, if he didn't need the car, he let me drive the 1932 Chevy to school, keep it all week and drive it home on Friday night.

After all the years I spent as a student, I found myself sitting behind the teacher's desk. I had been trained for the job and was anxious to start my new career. With only six pupils and three grades, I was lucky. If I remember right, the first year I had two 1st graders, two 4th graders and two 7th graders. We did everything the larger schools did. We pledged allegiance to the flag every morning, held classes in all the subjects, had spelling contests and arithmetic drills, and put on a little Christmas program for the parents and others who lived in the community.

Ormie started teaching at the Seymour School, which was about twenty miles north of my school. But he had signed up for the National Guard while in college and had to quit teaching when the Japanese bombed Pearl Harbor. President Roosevelt declared war on Japan and Ormie got orders to report immediately for duty at Camp Claiborne, Louisiana. We corresponded with letters, and when I dismissed my school for the summer, he asked me to come with his parents to Louisiana to visit him.

Overjoyed, I could hardly wait for his parents Dode and Clara, his brother Aldy, and Aldy's girlfriend Margo to pick me up. Margo and I were tickled we had matching playsuits to wear for the trip. They were red and white print with shorts and top to match. We made the 1,500- mile trip from South Dakota to Camp Claiborne, staying several nights in cabins along the way. Aldy, Margo and I had never seen a black person before, and somewhere in Arkansas we saw a little black boy sitting alongside the road eating a piece of watermelon almost bigger than he was; we stopped to talk to him.

"Do you mind if I take your picture?" I asked.

"As dirty as I is?" he asked. I wish I still had that picture but it burnt up in the fire we had in 1947, along with all our other pictures.

We had good times on the trip, even though one night Clara, Margo and I had to sleep in one bed and Aldy and Dode in another because we couldn't find a cabin with three beds. Also, one time when Aldy was driving through a little town, Dode yelled, "Stop the car! I see a purse on the side of the road." Aldy slammed on the brakes, Dode jumped out to pick up the purse, but just as he grabbed for it, some kids pulled it away on a string they had fastened to it.

"Darn kids!" Dode grumbled as he got back in the car.

When we finally arrived at Camp Claiborne, we found Ormie; he took us into the mess hall where he had already eaten his supper. We were hungry and something smelled awfully good. We were late for the meal but the cooks gave us each a big plate of spaghetti. Ormie lived at a farmhouse where his sister Gladys and her husband and little boy Max lived. They put us all up for the few nights we stayed.

One day Ormie and I took his folks' car and drove to Alexandria, Louisiana, the closest town to the base. He took me to a jewelry store where we picked out my diamond engagement ring. We drove to a nice little park and spread a blanket out on the grass to sit on while we talked. We hadn't had much time alone since I arrived.

Ormie took my hand. "Honey, will you be my wife when this war is over?"

"Yes, of course I will marry you," I answered. He took the ring out of his pocket and put it on my finger, and we embraced and kissed. We had talked of marriage many times before, but this time it was for real. We went back to the farm to tell everyone. It was a joyful time for us.

All eight of us—Dode and Clara, Aldy and Margo, Gladys and Max, and Ormie and I—piled in the folks' 1940 Ford four-door sedan to go to Mardi Gras in New Orleans. Max was only three years old and rode on the window ledge behind the backseat. We bought some crab and took it to a park to eat it; it was the first time most of us had ever eaten crab meat. I still love it, and whenever I eat it I think of that day in the park in New Orleans. We started back home late at night and all of us slept, except the drivers of course. Gladys did most of the driving, but when she got sleepy, Ormie took over for her.

When it was time to go home to South Dakota, I hated to tell my fiancé goodbye because I knew he would be shipping out before long; we didn't know where he would go or when we would see each other again.

On the road home Dode teased me, "Em, you're going to hurt your eyes looking at that ring all the way home."

I had signed a contract to teach another year at Beck School. This time I was offered more money ($65 a month), but my room and board was raised to $12 a month. When I got home from the trip to Louisiana, I buried myself in my work and enjoyed my job as a country school teacher.

Ormie was shipped off to Ireland and I had no idea when he would be back. One afternoon I dismissed my students, finished cleaning up the schoolroom and sat down at the piano to play awhile before walking home to Hiram and Mary's. I thought I heard someone in the cloakroom, stopped playing to listen, and heard the noise again.

"Surprise!" I heard someone holler. My mouth flew open and I squealed with delight when my sweetheart appeared from around the corner. I thought my guy was in Ireland, but there he was, within my reach. He grabbed me, and that was just the beginning of the many surprises I had in store for the rest of my life with this fun-loving man. He came back to the States for Officer Training and was granted a short furlough before reporting at Ft. Belvoir, Virginia. We had only the rest of the evening together, much too short a visit for two people in love. We would probably have to wait until the war ended to see each other again and make plans for our wedding.

When I finished my second year at Beck School, I had no idea what exciting things would happen in my life. That was the last time I ever sat behind a teacher's desk in a schoolroom.

~Chapter 2~
My Country Calls

Teaching school turned out to be a good experience for me. After working with my students and grading their report cards at the end of each period, I could see they had accomplished what I had set out for them to do. I especially enjoyed putting on a Christmas program. But after finishing two terms in the same place with only six pupils, I needed something more challenging.

I left South Dakota only once before at the age of nine, when May and I went with Mom and Dad to the west coast to visit relatives. Ruth had never left South Dakota and we both felt the need to spread our wings. My sweetheart was overseas; I didn't have any idea when he would come back.

When school dismissed in June of 1942, Ruth and I boarded a bus in Deadwood, South Dakota, bound for Denver, Colorado. We went there to spend some time helping my brother Bill and his wife Frances because they expected their second child. Their daughter Ann was just a toddler, and it was fun giving her a bath every day and playing with her while Frances was in the hospital. Bill went to work every day, so Ruth and I had the responsibility of the house besides taking care of Ann. When Frances came home with the new baby, Jeanie, I helped with her too.

We got accustomed to our duties at Bill and Frances's house and found we had time on our hands. One morning after we finished the dishes and house work, Frances suggested, "Why don't you girls get on the streetcar and go downtown? I think it would be fun for you to see what goes on in the city." Ruth and I agreed, and after Frances went with us once to show us the ropes, a couple times a week we hopped on the streetcar a block from Bill and Frances's house just to explore downtown Denver. Several times from the streetcar we saw a recruiting sign on a large building: WOMEN, JOIN THE ARMY. That sign seemed to beckon us, and the third time we saw it we started discussing it.

"Maybe we should check that out," Ruth said one morning.

"It would be a chance for us to do something for our country, and I don't think either of us is crazy about teaching school," I said.

Then Ruth said, "And it would give us a chance to see some of the rest of the world. Let's go see what it's about!" She pulled the cord to stop the streetcar.

I followed Ruth into the recruiting office that morning. Almost before we knew what happened, our teaching careers had come to an abrupt halt. Two green country girls from the sticks of South Dakota signed up for the duration of World War II. America was at war and we wanted to help.

Now I wondered if Ormie would like what I had done. Then Ruth and I began to wonder if our parents would approve. But my sister and I went ahead and took the written test, the first step in the enlisting process. We both passed, and that bolstered our confidence in what we had done.

When we reported for our physical examinations, we were in for a shock. Men and women went through this process at the same time, requiring us to walk up and down the halls from one examining room to another clad only in a thin robe opened down the back. We survived it, though, and Ruth and I both passed the physical. Too late to turn back, we were in the army now — the WAAC (Women's army Auxiliary Corps). The name later changed to WAC (Women's army Corps).

Recruits had to wait a month to six weeks for orders to

report for duty. Ruth and I had to go back home to await orders and to break the news to our family. The morning Bill took us to the bus in Denver, I asked him, "What do you think Dad will say about this?"

Bill said, "Oh, I don't really think you have to worry about that. He will probably be proud of you." But I still had misgivings because Dad had spent money on tuition to get us ready to be teachers.

On the bus on the way home I said to Ruth, "Boy, I sure hate to tell Dad, don't you?"

"Don't worry, I'll tell him," Ruth answered. She made me feel much better.

When the bus drove up to the depot, Dad was waiting for us when we got out. Mom waited in the car, and we loaded our suitcases and got in.

"We have news for you," Ruth told Mom and Dad right away. "Em and I have joined the women's army. We came home to wait for our orders to report for duty."

To my surprise Dad smiled and said, "I am very proud of you girls!" We already had three brothers in the military — Bill, Frank and Chris. I heard Dad boast to one of the neighbors, "Five of my kids are in the service of our country now."

I wrote to my fiancé Orman, who was stationed in Ireland, to ask his opinion about joining the WAAC. He wrote back, "No, I'd rather you wouldn't. I want you to stay the same sweet girl you are today." However, his answer arrived too late; I had already enlisted. Sometimes it took several months for his letters to arrive, or sometimes several came at once even though they were mailed at different times.

My orders to report for duty arrived before Ruth's. She traveled with me on the bus back to Denver to wait there for her orders. A week later, I boarded a train in Denver, a member of the first company of WAACs mobilized. I traveled with several other recruits on a troop train from Denver to Ft. Des Moines. It was my first time on a train, so I was a little apprehensive because I didn't have the slightest idea what lay ahead for me.

When the train arrived at the station in Des Moines, we new women recruits loaded into the back of a canvas-covered GI truck to be transported to Ft. Des Moines. We crowded in on the benches on each side of the truck box. We had male corporals, sergeants and company commander since we were the first company of women. When we got to the base, we were assigned to a huge barracks that looked like horse stables. We had no separate rooms — just long rows of bunks with a footlocker at the foot of each bed, and a small metal closet. There were no walls or partitions; each private had her "room" for as long as we remained at Ft. Des Moines. There we met women from all over the United States, most of whom arrived about the same time we did.

"What have I gotten myself into?" I muttered to myself when I saw the latrine at the back of the barracks. Inside there stood a long row of toilets with no partitions between them. No privacy whatsoever. The lavatories lined up along one wall, and the showers were in one big room with not even a shower curtain between them. Like it or not, in August of 1942, six weeks of basic training began in earnest.

The next morning I quickly found out this women's army was to be no vacation.

"Fall out!" the sergeant barked as the bugle call for reveille sounded at 5:00 a.m. We soon learned how to scramble to the latrine, get dressed, line up in orderly fashion, and stand at attention to salute our officers. The next surprise was 15 minutes of strenuous calisthenics. By the second morning we had plenty of sore muscles. But no time off and no excuses — we went through the same routine every morning. My habit of occasionally sleeping in vanished.

We marched to supply headquarters where we got measured and outfitted for our new military wardrobes. We shipped our civilian clothes home for the duration of the war.

Our new wardrobe consisted of one dress uniform with three each of skirts, shirts and jackets. The army issued each of us one pair of dress shoes, one pair of fatigue shoes, a dress hat, a fatigue hat, a purse, coveralls, several pairs of stockings, bras, underwear, pajamas, towels and washcloths. We had no color choices because everything was khaki, even the underwear. Only the fatigue dress was a brown- and white-striped seersucker fabric. We did our own laundry by hand in large tubs located in the latrine and hung it out to dry on clotheslines behind the barracks.

"Hup two, three, four," "right face," "left face," and "about face" we heard daily as we marched to and from classes and practiced marching drills. The first sergeant marched us everywhere we had to go on the post. I loved the marching drills; it was fun to show off our formations for visiting generals and other dignitaries. We once did our dress parade for President Franklin D. Roosevelt.

"Platoon, halt!" barked the sergeant. "Right face! Salute!"

All hands went up to salute as President Roosevelt was driven by slowly as he sat in the backseat of an open car. His dog Falla sat on the back of the car wagging his tail.

All WAACs attended classes in military courtesy, first aid, personal hygiene, map reading and current events. One day we marched to the infirmary for shots in both arms as we went through the line. Sore arms the next day didn't excuse us from calisthenics or drill practice.

I hoped to be assigned to clerical work after basic training, but to my disappointment, the army chose Cooks and Bakers School for me. Ruth was assigned to the motor pool and she chauffeured officers around the post or drove a truck into Des Moines after another truckload of recruits. I made the best of my assignment, however, and when I finished Cooks and Bakers School, I was promoted to the rank of sergeant.

I can laugh now at some of my experiences learning to cook, but at the time they embarrassed me. The first time I baked cakes (three huge sheet cakes), I got into the wrong bin and used salt in place of sugar; the mess officer suggested I make a powdered sugar frosting as thick as the cake with bananas in it to correct my mistake. The women devoured every piece.

When I had been at Ft. Des Moines for a few weeks, the first sergeant came to tell me I had a phone call. "You can take it on this pay phone here in the hall," he explained.

"Hi, honey, bet you can't guess where I am," Ormie said when I answered.

"I don't have the slightest idea. Are you in the States?" I said.

He answered, "Yes, and I'm right here in Des Moines. They sent me back to the States for reassignment. I am at Aunt Alice's house. She and Uncle Roy picked me up at the train depot; I have only this one night to stay here. Is there any chance you can get off base so we can spend a little time together?"

I said, "I'll see what I can do, but you and I both know I can't leave the base while I'm in basic training. I'll call you back later."

I hadn't seen Ormie since he surprised me in my schoolhouse the year before. When I told Emma Rose, my new friend, about my problem, she said, "Don't worry, I'm on duty tonight as CQ (Charge of Quarters) and I'll cover for you at bed check."

I called Ormie back. "I'm not sure I'm doing the right thing, honey, but I just have to see you, if only for an hour or two."

He came to pick me up with his Aunt Alice's car and took me to her house. After Aunt Alice and Uncle Roy went to bed we talked till about 4:00 in the morning. We were so much in love, and wished for the war to be over soon so we could start our life together and have a family.

But finally the hours were used up and I had to get back to camp before anyone discovered me missing. He took me back to my barracks, we kissed and hugged goodbye again, and I jumped into my bunk with my clothes on just in time to hear the bugle play reveille. I owed my friend and CQ a big debt of gratitude, and to this day I don't know what would have happened had I been caught. I think the only reason I got away with it was because Ormie had his lieutenant bars on his shoulders and the MPs (Military Police) who checked people in and out of the gate saw his bars, saluted him and were too intimidated to ask me who I was.

Four months passed, but it seemed like years. I learned a lot in that short time and kept busy. I was homesick my first time away from home, but when I got lonely, I walked down to Ruth's barracks in the evening to compare letters from home. army rules prohibited us going on weekend passes during basic training. We attended church services on the base on Sundays and walked to the PX (Post Exchange) to shop for personal items. We were also allowed to attend movies on the post.

I graduated from Cooks and Bakers School a full-fledged cook, ready for my next assignment in the army, wherever it might be.

Private Emma Ruby (Willey)

Lt. Orman Willey

~Chapter 3~

Ft. Oglethorpe or Bust

My orders came for transfer from Ft. Des Moines, so I walked down the street to see my sister.

I said, "Ruth, I hate to tell you I am leaving Ft. Des Moines. I've been transferred to Ft. Oglethorpe, Georgia." Excited about my new adventure, I had mixed feelings because I hated to leave Ruth behind. No more walking down to her barracks to exchange letters from home. I had to face my future without her, but it was another step in furthering my career.

"I'll miss you," Ruth said. "Please write when you get there." We hugged and parted company, not knowing how long it would be before we met again. After four months at Ft. Des Moines, I boarded a troop train headed to Georgia. I had received a promotion along with my transfer, and with staff sergeant stripes on my sleeves, I would report for mess sergeant duty at one of the three mess halls at Ft. Oglethorpe, where new recruits came in every day.

Our group of military women felt like pioneers. When we got off the train in Chattanooga, Tennessee, on January 3, 1943, we had new challenges to face as one of the first groups of women to open another base for the Women's army Corps. The weather was more like spring than winter, quite a change from Iowa's cold temperatures and snow. I would spend 20 months of my life at Ft. Oglethorpe, Georgia, across the Tennessee border from Chattanooga.

I took charge of my mess hall with the assistance of capable, assigned cooks. Every day we cooked for and fed up to 300 women new to military life. With my mess officer's help, I soon became accustomed to ordering the food from the commissary and organizing the cooks and KPs (Kitchen Police). I liked the challenge and soon my work became routine. I loved my job.

Maggie, one of my best friends at Ft. Oglethorpe, managed one of the other mess halls on base. She and I bunked side by side in our barracks. Several times we went to town together for the weekend, got a hotel room in Chattanooga and just relaxed. During the summer we ordered watermelons for the mess hall, and often carried a big one home to the barracks and sat out on the lawn to devour it. Melons being exceptionally good in Georgia, they made a wonderful treat after a hard day's work.

During the spring and summer months, several of us got together to go on hikes through the Civil War military park joining Ft. Oglethorpe. We saw interesting history about that war and the cannons and monuments for the battles fought there. The United States Congress authorized four military parks between 1890 and 1899 to preserve and commemorate battlefields, the largest of which was the Chickamauga and Chattanooga at Oglethorpe. The Campaign for Chattanooga was fought from June to November 1863.

Sometimes during the summer Maggie and I rode a bus to the top of Lookout Mountain and enjoyed the view; we could see for miles. We learned more about the history of the Civil War because that was where the "battle above the clouds" was fought, and is part of the Chickamauga and Chattanooga Military Park, which we hiked through at Ft. Oglethorpe.

We often had the opportunity to go to Chattanooga to concerts that were always free to the military. One show I enjoyed immensely was the Roy Acuff show, which included Minnie Pearl.

After serving my country for a year, I had earned a

furlough. Finally I could go home for the first time; this entailed a long train ride from Chattanooga, Tennessee, to Rapid City, South Dakota. When I boarded the train, it was packed with GIs, not an empty seat anywhere. Here I sat, one lonely WAC sitting on my suitcase in the middle of the aisle. Not one GI gave up his seat for a lady soldier. It was plain to see some of the male soldiers didn't approve of women in the military with them. Evident in town, too, a lot of civilians didn't respect women in uniform. They made remarks like, "Why didn't you stay home where you belong?" If a woman in the military became pregnant, she was promptly discharged. If she wanted to get married while in the service, she first had to get permission from her commanding officer. The women of World War II paved the way for the women of today to have careers in the military.

When I changed trains in Cincinnati, I got a seat on a train to Chicago, and from there to Rapid City. Getting off in Chicago to change trains, I handed my suitcase to a redcap thinking he would see me to the next train, but I lost him in the crowd. My suitcase was gone and all I had left was what I had in my purse. I inquired at the information booth and found my suitcase was in storage. It cost me a dollar to retrieve it. That taught me a valuable lesson: hang on to my own luggage.

Back on the train, I was finally on my way to Rapid City and home. The train chugged into town where I was happy to see Mom, Dad and May waiting for me at the depot. I loved being home for a few days, but while I was away, the big two-story house I had grown up in had shrunk. The rooms seemed tiny after living in a large army barracks for over a year. I enjoyed the time with my family, especially a good visit with my sister May. However, ten days later I was ready to go back to my military duties. All the hard work had been worthwhile. I had found my niche in the women's army and in the world. I went back to the routine of the mess hall.

One night Ormie called. "I'm back in the States again, honey. How are you?"

"I'm just fine now that I know where you are," I answered. "What's coming up next for you?"

"I think it's about time we start making plans for our wedding," he said. "We're only about 500 miles apart and we could meet each other on weekend passes once in a while," he added.

"Do you suppose we could get our furloughs at the same time and get married in South Dakota?"

"That's a great idea," Ormie said, and we began making plans to meet in June in South Dakota for our long-awaited wedding.

Personal priorities then took precedence over army business, and our wedding plans began to take shape. First, I applied for a furlough and learned that before I could get married I had to ask permission from my company commander. At 23, I couldn't see how anyone could possibly object (or even have the right to). But I went through the necessary channels, marched to company headquarters, walked in, and gave the CC my best salute as I stood at attention.

"At ease, Sergeant," the captain said.

"Captain, ma'am, I am asking permission to be married while I am home on furlough in June," I said.

"Are you sure you are old enough to take this step?" she asked.

"Yes, ma'am, I certainly do," I said. After a few more questions, the CC handed me a paper she had signed that granted permission for the marriage.

"Thank you, ma'am," I said as I quickly saluted, did a fast about-face and left. I had my permission in hand, but it was the most intimidating thing I ever did in my life. I hope the army has discontinued that practice.

Ormie and I managed to get our furloughs at the same time; he left from Camp Claiborne and I from Ft. Oglethorpe. We planned to meet in Chicago and go home together. This time the long trip home on the train meant I would marry the man I loved. I arrived in Chicago thinking I would find Ormie around every corner. I wondered if I would know him because I hadn't seen him for so long. I thought every man I saw in uniform must be my man, but no such luck. Finally I had him paged, but still didn't find him. I barely made it to my next train on time and went home without him.

~CHAPTER 4~
STUCK IN THE CREEK —
OUR WEDDING DAY

I finally made it home for my furlough. This time my brother Richard met me at the train in Rapid City and drove me home to Spring Creek Farm. We had a good visit on the way home, and when I greeted Mom, Dad and May it was good to see they all looked in good health. But the trip home this time was to meet my sweetheart and finally have our wedding. I had to find out where he was.

"Have you heard anything about Ormie?" I asked.

"Yes, we heard he got home yesterday," Dad said.

Immediately I went to the phone and cranked out Ormie's parents' rings. His mother Clara answered the phone.

"I heard Ormie got home yesterday. Is he there?" I asked.

"Yes, I'll get him for you," Clara said. I waited anxiously for him to get to the phone.

"Hello, honey," I said. "When did you get home?"

"Yesterday. Where were you in Chicago?" he said.

"I was there, even tried to page you. Where were you?"

"Well, honey, I tried to page you too and finally decided you must have gone on home without me," Ormie said. "It really doesn't matter, we're both home now, so let's get the show on the road."

"Okay, but when will I get to see you?"

"How about tomorrow? I'll come down right after breakfast in the morning and we'll have all day to make our plans."

I agreed, and after more conversation we said good night. I went to bed that night feeling relieved that we had finally made connections, and dropped off to sleep dreaming of his visit the next day. We had a lot of catching up to do.

When Ormie drove into the yard in his Packard, I ran out to meet him. We hugged and kissed over and over. In the house, he greeted my family and then we sat in the living room and talked, making final plans for our wedding. First we asked my sister May to be my bridesmaid and then Ormie called her boyfriend Cliff to ask him to be his best man. We didn't have much time because we both had to get back in camp in ten days. So the next day we made a trip to Bison to get our marriage license at the court house. Then we stopped to make arrangements with Reverend Solberg to officiate at the ceremony. From there we went to Lemmon, South Dakota, to purchase our wedding rings for our double ring ceremony. I found a pretty dress for my bridesmaid. My memory tells me it was navy blue with a white lace collar and cuffs. Ormie and I would speak our vows in our army uniforms because we weren't allowed to wear civilian clothes as long as the war was on. We set the wedding date for June 12, and May's boyfriend Cliff agreed to bring May and me to the Willey house on the 12th.

"I'll see you in a couple days, honey," Ormie said, and he kissed me and got back in his car and drove back to his parents' house. We both visited with our families for the next couple days.

It rained cats and dogs on June 11 and I woke up on my wedding day to find it still raining hard. May and I didn't expect Cliff to come after us because of all the rain, but here he came, plowing mud into the yard with his 1938 Chevy coupe, coming the seven miles from his house. People who lived in those times without hard-surfaced roads always referred to driving on the dirt roads when it rained as "plowing mud." As May explained at our 50th anniversary party, "It would be a gross understatement to say the roads were hard-surfaced in 1943."

I said to Cliff, "I wonder if we should even try to make the trip in this muddy mess."

"It's my job to get you to the altar," Cliff teased with a grin. "We can take to the prairie if the road is too muddy. You girls willing to give it a try?"

"Of course!" I said, and May and I ran upstairs to get our coats and my suitcase I had already packed early that morning. Away we went, trying to miss the worst mud holes by driving out on the prairie as Cliff had suggested.

Things went quite well until the little coupe started heating and we had to find water to cool it down. After all that rain, every low spot on the prairie had water standing in it, so we dipped up a canful to pour into the radiator. We let the Chevy cool off and started out again. Several times we got into mud and May and I had to get out and give the car a little push to get it going again. There I was in my wedding outfit, my once-clean uniform, splashed with mud, and my shoes a muddy mess, too. I hoped I would be able to clean up before the ceremony.

Finally we made it to the turnoff to the Willey ranch and thought we had it made. But we had to cross Rabbit Creek to get to the ranch, and it was full of water and running rapidly. We wondered if we should try to cross it.

"We'll give it a try. We can't quit now," Cliff said. He stepped on the gas and headed across the running creek, but the engine got wet, and there we were, sitting in the middle of the creek with water running over our feet. We had to bail out and walk the rest of the way.

Ormie and his family hadn't heard us come. When we got close to the house, the dog began barking at us, and Ormie and his parents came out of the house to welcome us.

May and I took off our stockings, washed them out and hung them up to dry. I sponge-cleaned my uniform because it was the only wedding dress I had. We wiped off our shoes and set them by the stove to dry. To this day Orman teases me, "I thought I was safe when it rained so hard that day, but you waded the creek to get me."

My future father-in-law Dode hitched up a team of horses, fastened a log chain to the bumper of Cliff's Chevy and pulled it out of the creek. While it dried out along with our shoes and stockings, my future mother-in-law fixed a nice lunch for everyone. When it was time, we got into Orman's 1941 Packard and headed for the county seat, with May and Cliff following close behind in the Chevy.

We spoke our vows on June 12, 1943, in a little Lutheran church in Bison, South Dakota, with the Reverend Clarence Solberg officiating. The only people present were the minister, the best man Cliff and bridesmaid May, and Ormie and I, bride and groom. Clad in our army uniforms, we had no flowers, no music, no guests—just a simple ceremony that made us husband and wife. The vows we spoke that day have lasted for over sixty years. Because of the war, it almost didn't happen, but I am positive it was meant to be.

May ended her talk at our 50th wedding celebration with these words: "I remember the marriage. It was unique and special. My sister Emma and her sweetheart Orman—both in officers' uniforms, answering the call of their country, pausing just a moment to begin their life together. And the two were made one...and to go again separately to serve in the war."

We left for a five-day honeymoon, which took us back to our respective military posts. We plowed more mud from Bison to Buffalo, even had to ask some people to help us out of the mud in one place. When we got to Buffalo we drove on the gravel road, and from there it was smooth sailing to Belle Fourche.

We rented a room in the Hampton Hotel, the largest hotel in town. It was a noisy place but we spent our first night together there. We both took showers and I got into my new blue nightgown and robe I had purchased for the occasion. The army wasn't going to tell me to wear my khaki pajamas on my wedding night. It had been a long wait to be together, but it was worth it to finally have a little time to get acquainted with no interruptions from anyone.

The next morning we walked around the corner to a restaurant for breakfast and then started on our way east and south. We stopped in Piedmont to visit Ormie's brother Noble and his wife Margie for a few minutes, and in Rapid City for a short visit with his other brother Aldy and his wife Margo.

In wartime we had to have coupons for gas and tires. We started east from Rapid City and hadn't gone many miles when we had a flat tire. Ormie changed the tire for the spare, got back in the car and said, "I think we'll have to have a new tire. The spare isn't a very good one and we have a long trip ahead of us."

"What'll we do?" I asked. "We don't have any coupons for tires, just gas." We stopped at a service station and filled up with gas.

"I had a flat back there a few miles, and I really need a new tire and have no coupons. Is there any way you could sell me a tire?"

The station operator saw we were both in uniform, and when he found out how far we had to go to get back to camp, he said, "I'll make an exception in this case. Thanks for fighting this darn war for all of us."

Filled up with gas and with a new tire in the trunk, we started out again.

In every little town we drove through, this new husband of mine whistled at any females on the street. I guess he wanted to see my reaction, and sometimes it wasn't too nice. I finally realized he was just teasing me. This man would do most anything for fun.

We stopped in Des Moines and spent one night with Aunt Alice and Uncle Roy. The next morning we went to a portrait studio and had our wedding pictures taken before we headed south for Georgia. We stayed in motels the rest of the way, and by the time we got to Ft. Oglethorpe, we knew each other well.

Once again, we had to say goodbye. I was back at my post in Georgia and Ormie had to report to Camp Claiborne. We wondered how long it would be before we saw each other again, but hoped to meet on weekends when we could arrange passes to meet halfway somewhere. The war in Europe was getting intense; American troops were invading

1943 Wedding Picture

Belgium and Germany and our future was extremely uncertain.

Ormie called me the next day. "I have orders to leave for Germany right away," he said.

"Oh, no!" I said. "All those plans we made to meet on weekends will never happen now, will they?" I couldn't believe my ears.

"I'm afraid you're right, honey, at least not for a long time. We'll just have to wait till this darn war is over, and then we'll make up for lost time." We never laid eyes on each other till more than two years later after the war ended.

~Chapter 5~

Back to the Barracks

My new husband was sent overseas again—this time to Germany. So I buried myself in my work at Ft. Oglethorpe and prayed the war would soon end so we could be together again. Winter came and my name came up on a list for overseas service in Germany. Thrilled it might be a chance for me to see Ormie, I applied for a 10-day furlough before going overseas. I found myself on the train again, headed for South Dakota and home. But while there, a blizzard made roads impassable and I couldn't get to the train depot ninety miles away. I phoned company headquarters for an emergency extension of my furlough. When I finally arrived back in camp, someone else had been sent to Germany in my place. I had lost an opportunity to see Europe, but worse, I wouldn't get to see my husband anytime soon.

A break in routine helped soothe my disappointment. I went on temporary assignment as mess sergeant on a troop train from Ft. Oglethorpe to Stockton, California, where three cooks and I prepared meals on the train for soldiers who were being transferred. We spent one night in Stockton and from there made a trip to Chinatown in San Francisco. Mission accomplished, the next morning we boarded the train again and had a relaxing trip back to Ft. Oglethorpe, back to our regular duties at the mess hall.

Two months later, new orders came for my transfer to Dow Field at Bangor, Maine. The army kept my life interesting and I loved the chance to see more of our country. Ready for a new adventure, I boarded another train. A 10-day delay-in-route in Washington, DC, gave me a welcome vacation. I met and made new friends, Margaret and Casey, who went to Dow Field with me as my first cooks. We took the bus into Washington, DC, several times to take in the sights of our nation's capital. We walked all the way up the steps of the Washington Monument, spent several hours in the Smithsonian Institute, and saw the Capitol building, the White House, the Pentagon and the Lincoln Memorial. We took a bus tour to Mount Vernon, the preserved home of George Washington, an interesting taste of our nation's history. I got a lump in my throat and I was proud to be a member of the Women's army Corps. It made me realize I had an important role to play in serving my country.

Reporting-in day at Dow Field brought a pleasant surprise. Margaret, Casey and I were assigned to a private room to share. It was the first time any of us had any kind of privacy since joining the WAC. No more living in open barracks. We had it made. Now we were in the Women's Air Force because Dow Field was an air base.

My job as mess sergeant at Dow Field was easier than working with recruits at Oglethorpe. I managed the mess hall, planned meals with the GI menus, and had many of the same responsibilities I'd had at Ft. Oglethorpe. I had the assistance of my capable first cooks and other well-trained personnel. The army supplied me with menus (which I had the authority to change if needed). The menus were varied, anything from ovens full of roast beef, roast pork, baked ham, pork chops, hamburger, you name it. They were balanced meals, and for dessert we made our own cakes, pies and cookies.

Once a week, a GI picked me up in an army truck and drove me to the commissary to pick up groceries for the week. I carried quarters of beef, crates of frozen chicken, heavy cases of canned goods and 100-pound sacks of potatoes, sugar and flour and loaded them into the truck. When we got back to the mess hall, the KPs helped me unload the truck and carry everything into the mess hall.

I helped with some of the cooking, especially cutting up meats. We had learned how to cut up a quarter of beef, a whole hog, chickens and turkeys in Cooks and Bakers School back at Ft. Des Moines, so the training came in handy. The chickens came frozen and whole, with the entrails intact. While still frozen, we whacked them in two with a meat cleaver, cleaned out the insides, then quartered and washed them, ready for the grill or the oven.

My work soon became a matter of routine, and my biggest challenge was keeping the mess hall clean and dishes and silverware squeaky clean, because we never knew when the inspecting officer would pop in to run his white-gloved hand over everything.

The women stationed at Dow Field were assigned to this base permanently for the duration of the war, and the 200 women who ate at the mess hall worked elsewhere on the base. Many times business was slow at the mess hall on weekends because some people left on weekend passes. On Sunday nights the menu often consisted of sandwiches and a relish tray with pickles, olives, radishes, etc., and fruit or ice cream.

When we had time off we rode the bus to Bangor for a day, an evening or sometimes a weekend. Other nights we girls went to the NCO (Non-Commissioned Officers) Club, shared a pitcher of beer, and when we had music, danced with the GIs. A theater on post made it convenient to take in the latest movie. On Sundays, Catholic and Protestant church services were available.

Margaret and I became good friends and went everywhere together. One weekend she and I got a weekend pass and hitched a ride on a B-17 to Goose Bay, Newfoundland. It didn't cost anything for the ride, and we visited another military base there. I don't remember much about it except we got to see some different country and we needed a break from our routine duties at the mess hall. We often went to town on the weekend to stay in a hotel, take in a movie and eat in a restaurant. I especially liked Maine lobster, and ate in a Chinese restaurant for the first time in my life. We tried them all, but the seafood was the best. Bangor is where I first tasted lobster, and I would love to go back there and have it again because I've never had it anywhere as good.

Once Margaret and I saw a sign for a palm reader, and just for fun we went in to see what we could find out about our futures. I took off my wedding ring to see if I could fool her. The palm reader took us one at a time into her darkened room. As she read the lines in my palm, she talked.

"You have two brothers in the service, and I think one of them is Frank. Is that true?"

"Yes, it is," I answered. "But what do you see in my future?"

"You are married to a young man who has light-colored hair, blue eyes and is very handsome. He is in the service right now and is a long way from you. When he comes home, I see three children for you." I hadn't fooled her at all, or else she was a good guesser. Everything she told me came true; however, Margaret didn't find the same, as her predictions of a pending marriage never happened.

One weekend one of the cooks invited several of us to go home with her to her home in Maine. Her family lived in a large, sprawling farmhouse with the barn attached to one end of the house. Most of the farms in New England were like that, while the barns on the prairie in South Dakota stood separate from the house. We enjoyed some home-cooked food her mother made, and a weekend in the country gave us another welcome break from our duties at the mess hall. Another weekend Margaret, Casey and I packed our bathing suits and took a bus to Bar Harbor, where we swam in the salty water, something else I had never experienced on the prairie.

My military career was about to end, but I didn't know it at that time. Rumors told us the war's end would come soon, but I hadn't heard it from my husband yet. Every day we listened to the radio intently, hoping to hear the good news.

~CHAPTER 6~
WORLD WAR II ENDS

"Extra! Extra! Extra! The war is over!" We heard the news repeatedly on the radio.

"I think it's time to celebrate," I said to my roommates. "I'm sure Ormie will be on his way home soon."

Margaret and Casey both agreed. Since we usually went there on Saturday night, we took off for the NCO Club. We ordered a pitcher of beer and lifted our glasses to toast the end of the war.

The sergeant in charge came over to our table and said, "Willey, there's a phone call for you. You can take it in the next room."

"Who could be calling me?" I asked. I hoped there wasn't someone sick at home, and I went to answer the call.

"Hello, honey," the voice at the other end said.

"Is it really you, Ormie?"

"It's really me. How are you?"

"I'm fine! You surprised me! I didn't expect to hear from you yet. Where are you anyway?"

"I'm in New York City, en route to Sparta, Wisconsin, to be mustered out of the army. The war ended while we were on the way back for reassignment to the Pacific. Can you put in for a furlough and meet me in Sparta?" Ormie asked.

"I'll be there as soon as I can make it. Don't leave till I get there," I said.

"Okay, I'll see you there as soon as you can make it. I can't wait to get you in my arms again."

"Me too, honey, I'll be in Sparta as soon as I can." We said good night and I went back to the girls at the table. Now I had a better reason to celebrate.

The next morning I made arrangements for a furlough, and that night I boarded the train, Wisconsin-bound. Ormie and I hadn't seen each other in more than two years, not since our short honeymoon. I don't remember for sure how long it took to get to Sparta by train from Bangor, but I think it took all night and most of the next day. It seemed like forever, but finally the train chugged into the little depot. I got off the train expecting Ormie to be there to meet me. But he wasn't there. What would I do? I sat down to collect my wits and waited awhile, but finally decided to go to town and get a room because he was probably tied up getting his mustering-out orders. I hailed a taxi and went into the little town.

"Is there a hotel in town?" I asked.

The taxi driver said, "Lady, where do you think you're going to stay in this town? A whole trainload of GIs came in here yesterday and I doubt if the hotel has any rooms left, but you can check it out." I paid him and got out at the hotel.

"Sorry, Sergeant, but our rooms are all taken. But there's a private home down the street that might have a room left," the clerk said. He gave me directions to get there. Nothing to do but get a room and hope Ormie would find me. I picked up my suitcase and started walking down the street looking for the address the clerk gave me when I heard someone yell.

"Hey, wait for me!" It was Ormie. "Where do you think you're going?"

"I'm trying to find a place to spend the night with you," I said. As I dropped the suitcase, he grabbed me and we embraced and kissed each other right there in the middle of the street. We continued walking to the house and they still had a room upstairs. Our long-awaited reunion began, and civilian life would start as soon as I got my discharge. After we caught up on loving and had a good visit, we realized we hadn't eaten, so Ormie pulled on his clothes and went out to find us something to eat. He came back with a couple hamburgers and two cans of beer, and we had our first meal together since he'd left me at Ft. Ogelthorpe after our honeymoon.

We caught the train the next morning to Minneapolis. Ormie had his discharge in hand, but I still had to go back to Dow Field to await my orders. We spent the night in Minneapolis. We met Ormie's buddy Alvin and his wife Opal at a restaurant and had dinner together. They hadn't seen each other either since the guys went overseas.

The next morning we bought a plane ticket to fly home to Rapid City. After visiting both of our families for about ten days, we took the train back to Bangor, Maine, and Dow Field to await my orders. I would be mustered out of the army at Ft. Des Moines, Iowa, the same place where this adventure began three long years earlier.

We still had some time before my furlough ended, and we stayed all night in Chicago en route to Bangor. We got a room in a big hotel in downtown Chicago, where we could walk to a restaurant for dinner. We needed to have some time alone together after visiting relatives for ten days. We found a nice restaurant close to the hotel, and I'll never forget what I had for dinner: Shrimp Newberg, something I had never eaten before. It was delicious. Ormie ordered a bottle of wine and it was our second honeymoon celebration. While we ate our dinner, a photographer came and asked if we wanted our picture taken, and we let him take one. I treasured that picture until it burned up with all our other pictures a few years later. We finished our celebration by having room service the next morning, breakfast in bed.

When we arrived in Bangor, we rented a small apartment for about a week while waiting for my orders.

When we left Dow Field for the last time, we hitchhiked on a C-47 airplane to an airfield in New Hampshire, where we caught another ride on a B-17 bound for Detroit, Michigan. The ride in the cargo compartment was the scariest time of my military career. We just nicely got airborne when the pilot started maneuvering the plane in different directions and tipping the wings. Suddenly we knew something was amiss.

The co-pilot appeared from the cockpit and said, "You two will have to put on these parachutes just in case of an emergency landing." He said there was a leak one of the wing tanks, and when we looked out the window we could see the gasoline spraying on the window. Jumping from a plane with a parachute on was not something I had ever dreamed about doing.

"You'll have to pull the cord for me because if I jump out of this plane, I'll probably pass out!" I said to Ormie. Thank God the pilot was experienced, and by maneuvering around he was able to circle and land back on the airstrip. They discovered the cap on one gas tank hadn't been securely fastened. They checked everything out and we boarded the same plane again. Landing safely in Detroit, we had enough of flying and got on the train again to head for Ft. Des Moines. It didn't take long for me to get my discharge from the army, and we were finally free to go home and start our own life adventure together.

I had a lifetime of experiences in three years, and even though I was happy about getting out into civilian life again, I missed the regimen of the army. The last time I heard TAPS I was walking across the field from the mess hall to the barracks. When the bugle rang out, I stopped, stood at attention and saluted the United States flag as I had done so many times in the past three years. When the bugle rang out the last time for me, I felt a little sad as patriotism tugged at my heart. Looking back, I wouldn't take a million for my loving husband and my three beautiful children, but I'm glad I had the WAC experience first.

~CHAPTER 7~
OUR "PUNKIN" ARRIVES

Finally Ormie and I both had our discharges in hand and had some decisions to make. He found it difficult to decide if he wanted to be a rancher and farmer. He had acquired a few head of cattle during the war after his brother RC passed away in 1942. He bought the small herd of nine cows from Letha, RC's widow. His father Dode took care of the cattle until we got home. Ormie decided to find a temporary job and work for a while. He left his cattle on the ranch, where his dad continued caring for them with his own herd. We rented a small apartment in Rapid City in back of the house where Aldy and Margo lived. My husband got a job working at a filling station.

We got nicely settled in our little apartment. I enjoyed going to the grocery store to get staples for my cupboards and prepare to cook for the two of us. What a difference from cooking for 200 or more.

I had everything any woman could ask for except for one thing: I wanted a baby. The second month after we got out of the army I missed my period. Could I be pregnant already? I couldn't wait to find out and made an appointment to see Margo's Dr. Jernstrom. After examining me, he said, "Yes, you are three months pregnant." His examination was painful, but since it was my first pregnancy, I didn't know what to expect. Elated, I couldn't wait to tell Ormie the good news. He had warned me before we got married that he might never be able to father children because of the bad case of mumps he had as a teenager. We both got excited about our future with a baby of our own, and we made so many plans that night we had trouble getting to sleep.

The next morning Ormie kissed me goodbye and went to work at the filling station. I had plans to do some cooking that day and make a batch of cookies for him before he came home. But it wasn't to be. He had barely left the house when I started bleeding. The blood gushed out of me and I got up long enough to fold up a sheet to put under me to keep from soiling the whole bed. Every time I moved, there was more blood. I didn't have the foggiest idea what was happening to me, but I knew I had to get help. Aldy and Margo had left for the weekend and I was in the house alone. We didn't have our phone in yet. The only thing to do was stay in bed and lie still, trying not to move and waiting for my sweetie to come home for lunch.

When Ormie opened the door and found me still in bed, he knew something was wrong. "What's wrong, honey?" he asked. When I told him, he hurried next door immediately to call the doctor.

"Doctor," he said, "my wife has been bleeding since this morning. What should we do?"

"You get her to the hospital as quickly as possible," he said.

I put on all the pads I could find and Ormie put stack of towels in the seat of the car for me to sit on. When we got in the hospital, I stood at the counter bleeding while I filled out admission papers. Finally they put me to bed.

"You have had a miscarriage," the doctor said. "We will do an operation to clean up the uterus, and you will be here about three days."

I couldn't believe it. Ormie and I were devastated. I remember being so angry with the lady in the bed next to me because she had labor pains and constantly I heard her complain, "Darn you, Cecil, this is all your fault!"

Finally I told her, "You should be thankful you're having a baby because I lost mine."

I remained in the hospital for three days and then went home to recuperate. It was the day before Thanksgiving and we didn't feel like joining the family for the holiday. Ormie said, "You don't have to cook either," and he took me out to the Virginia Café for Thanksgiving dinner. We never knew what caused the miscarriage, but I have always believed it happened because of the pelvic exam the doctor did the day before. We wanted a family, so we never stopped trying to get pregnant.

Not long after the loss of what would have been our first child, Ormie came home one day and asked, "How'd you like to go to Oregon to visit my sister Bonnie? I'm taking a leave of absence for a few weeks."

"Of course, I'd love to go, honey," I said. His other sister Gladys lived in Sturgis, South Dakota, and wanted to go to California to join her husband Jack, who was working out there after the war. We still had our 1941 Packard Ormie had stored in the barn on the ranch during the war. We packed our luggage and picked up Gladys with her two kids, Max and Bonnie Karen, and took off for Oregon and California. We had a good visit in Hillsboro, Oregon, with Bonnie and Russ before we went to San Francisco to find Jack. Gladys and the kids stayed there and we returned to Rapid City by ourselves. It was like another honeymoon.

When we got back, the tenants had moved out of the house behind our apartment while we were gone. We had our eye on it, and moved into the little furnished one-bedroom house. It was perfect for us because we had more room, so we decided to invite the Willey family for Christmas dinner. Aunt Alice was at the ranch visiting Dode and Clara. She came from Iowa to spend the winter. The invitations went out and they all came: Dode, Clara and Aunt Alice from the ranch, Aldy and Margo from next door, and Noble and Marge from Piedmont.

I was excited about fixing dinner for all my new relatives, so we bought a turkey and all the trimmings for the holiday meal.

Aunt Alice slept on the couch in our little house, and was on hand to help me. Everything went very well until I served the turkey the next day. Everyone had gone through our cafeteria line for their first helping of food. I went back to the kitchen to carve more turkey when Aldy sneaked out there to get more mashed potatoes and gravy. He whispered, "Em, did you know you forgot to clean the gizzard?" Mortified, I remembered that Aunt Alice had gotten up early and stuffed the bird before I got up that morning. She stuck in the gizzard, liver, and heart; I assumed she had cleaned it. She no doubt thought I had already done that.

"Don't worry, Em," Aldy said, "I won't say anything and nobody will know the difference. Your dressing is delicious." I quickly tossed the gizzard into the garbage can. Bless his heart, Aldy never told our secret, and to this day no one else heard about it, but you can be sure this turkey's face was red.

Early in the spring of 1946, Ormie had a chance to go on a construction job with a large construction company. They would start him out at $2.00 an hour, big wages in those days. We gave up our furnished apartment and packed everything we owned into the Packard. We moved to Ft. Peck, Montana, where he ran one of the huge terra cobra machines to help build the big earth dam there.

Our apartment at Ft. Peck was one of four in an old barracks that had been remodeled. We went to the secondhand store and bought a bed, table and chairs. The kitchen had a few cupboards but we used apple boxes for dresser drawers because we knew it was a temporary job. I made my curtains out of crepe paper. Our good friends John and Esther Fuller lived in an apartment in the other end of the barracks. We had fun playing cards with them and others; Whist was the favorite game. We met other lifelong friends there: Ray and Esther Shepherd and their three kids.

I was pregnant again, and went to Glasgow to see a doctor. We looked forward to having our baby in December, but we had all summer to wait while Ormie worked at his job on the dam. Esther was pregnant too and we took turns driving to Glasgow every month for our checkups. We both had the same doctor and made our appointments on the same day.

The Missouri River was a wonderful place to fish for walleye pike, and before I knew it, my husband got hooked on fishing every weekend. He urged me to go with him and I could see if I didn't I would be a fishing widow. I tagged along, and about the third time I went with him, I started catching fish. I got hooked too and we had many fun times on the river, packing a lunch and staying most of the day on weekends. The tiny town of Ft. Peck didn't offer much else to do for entertainment.

Fort Peck Dam is 21,430 feet long and 250 feet high. It is one of the world's largest earth-filled dams, built in the 1930s and '40s as a flood control and navigation improvement project. It is used for irrigation and hydroelectricity and is also a popular recreation area. Fort Peck Reservoir is 189 miles long and is one of the largest artificial lakes in the United States.

Once while Ormie was running his terra cobra over the miles of earth to build the dam, the foreman warned him and the other drivers, "The first one of you guys to run over one of those stakes will be fired." Well, guess what, Ormie did just that and the foreman came over to him and said, "Willey, you're fired for three days. Go take a little vacation."

We decided to go to Calgary in Canada to see the stampede rodeo. We had a good time; it was our first rodeo together and also the first carnival. When we got back to Ft. Peck, his job was waiting for him and he worked there until the job was done.

Early in the fall, work on the dam was finished. We threw away our crepe paper curtains, sold the furniture back to the secondhand store, loaded up our personal belongings and headed for the ranch. Ormie received several raises during the six months he worked and was making $3.00 an hour by the time the job ended; we saved $2,000 in six months. He decided he had enough of working for other people and would go into partnership with his dad, combining some farming with the cattle business.

We went back to Rapid City only until hunting season ended in the Black Hills. I stayed with Margo while the two brothers went hunting. We bought our 23-foot house trailer, and after they used it for their hunting trip, we moved out to the ranch and parked it next to the ranch house where Dode and Clara lived. They took a trip to Oregon to visit relatives for the winter and we stayed on the ranch to take care of the cattle until they returned in the spring. Since we were going to be ranchers, we traded the Packard for a brand new 1946 one-ton Ford pickup. The Packard brought a trade-in allowance of $1,000, the price Ormie had paid for it during the war.

My baby was growing inside me, and we knew that before Christmas it would be there. On December 2, I began to have some pains, and we decided to go south as far as May and Cliff's, stay all night and go on to Rapid City the next day, where I would enter the hospital. We didn't get to spend the night because my water broke, and we didn't waste much time getting on the road. Ormie checked the tires on our pickup and found one low, so he and Cliff quickly changed it. We will never forget how nervous Cliff and May were to get us going. They had experienced this only six weeks before when they went to the hospital to get their baby girl Bonita May, and worried we wouldn't get to the hospital in time.

About 11:00 p.m. we pulled in to the hospital. I was admitted and had labor pains all night. It was a good thing we hadn't waited until morning to come because on December 3, 1946, about 7:00 in the morning, Valerie Faye was born. She weighed 6 lb. 15 oz and was 19 inches long. Just after she arrived, I looked out of the window and saw the rising sun in the east. I will never forget my feeling of gratitude. I had a new daughter, she had ten fingers and ten toes, and she wriggled in my arms as much as to tell me, "I'm here." If I ever had any doubt about an existing God, it wasn't there anymore. How else could I have gotten this beautiful little girl? She was so precious to me and still is to this day. She got her nickname from her Daddy, our Punkin', and he still calls her that today.

I stayed in the hospital five days, which was the practice in those days, flat on my back. They brought my meals, and the nurses bathed me in bed and brought my baby to breastfeed every four hours. Ormie went to the ranch to take care of the cattle. After five days, he came to pick up Valerie and me to take us home to the ranch. It was winter, and we had over a hundred miles to travel. I brought a wardrobe for my new daughter to go home in with plenty of blankets, and I wrapped her up well to take her home.

When we arrived home, the house was cold because no one was there to keep the fires going. On a cold, snowy day out there on the prairie, I carried Valerie into the freezing house. I laid her on the bed and pulled the blanket back off her face, and she opened her eyes wide and looked around. I could almost hear her say, "Where am I?"

"What am I to do with this beautiful little creature?" I said to myself. I never had any training for this, but I loved her so much. Valerie was a fussy, colicky baby and I learned fast. I tried in vain to nurse her, but as soon as I started her on the formula the doctor gave me, she did better. She gave us a few evenings of walking the floor first, though.

The next day, Ormie saddled up his horse and went out to the pasture to check the cattle, so here I was alone with a little baby I scarcely knew what to do with. One thing I knew for sure, I had to do some laundry because the diapers were piling up; no such thing as Pampers then. That morning before her Daddy left he filled the boiler on the coal stove with water from the well. He left and I proceeded to do the laundry, even to hanging them outside on the clothesline to freeze dry. We didn't have dryers then either. But amazingly, it got done that way every week. Instinct served me well because Valerie gained weight and grew normally.

When Dode and Clara came home in the spring, we moved out into our little house trailer. It didn't have a bathroom, but neither did the ranch house. We used the outhouse and thought nothing of it. I kept the diaper pail in the little entry Ormie had built onto our trailer until washday. We survived the winter, and in early April Dode and Orman made plans for planting their crops of grain.

Orman at Ft. Pec, Montana

~CHAPTER 8~
THE FIRE

Ormie and Dode moved their tractor and other machinery to another farm they leased, ready to plant their crops and planning for a big harvest in the fall. The snow had melted but the cold March winds still blew across the prairie. Valerie and I spent the days in the house with Grandma Clara, because she had phlebitis in one leg and her doctor told her she must use crutches to walk and elevate her leg whenever possible. I took Valerie's baby basket in the house so I could keep a close eye on her while I helped Grandma with cooking, cleaning or whatever needed done.

Before the men left the ranch with the machinery, Ormie carried water from the well so I could do laundry for the family. The men would be gone all day seeding a field of flax. Valerie was five months old now. I gave her a bath before I started doing laundry and put her in her basket in the bedroom for a nap. By that time my wash water was hot, I filled the washer and rinse tubs and started the laundry. When I finished hanging the clothes on the clothesline to dry in a stiff breeze, I emptied the wash water, cleaned up the mess, and went into the living room to sit down with Grandma and relax awhile before starting dinner.

"It's not very warm in here, is it?" Clara asked.

"It sure isn't," I said.

"Must be soot built up in the chimney again," Clara said. She picked up a stove iron and tapped on the stovepipe to knock the soot loose, as she had done many times before. She soon had a roaring hot fire and the two of us settled down for a comfortable rest.

"What's that noise, Grandma?" I said.

"Sounds like an old rat gnawing up there in the attic," she answered. We both heard a scratching sound from upstairs in the old sod house. The sound got louder and I decided to investigate. Just as that thought crossed my mind, I saw smoke and debris flying past the living room window. I ran outside to discover the entire roof was ablaze. My heart sank. The scratching sound we had heard was the sound of a crackling fire. The roof had wooden shingles and they burned rapidly.

"The house is on fire!" I screamed as I rushed back into the house. My first thought was my baby. I grabbed Valerie, threw a blanket around her, ran to the car and put her in the backseat. I quickly scurried back into the house to help Grandma out, but she was already on her way out without her crutches. Baby and Grandma safely situated in the car, I knew it was useless to try to get help as we didn't have a phone and by that time the whole roof was a raging inferno. It was up to me if anything was going to be saved.

"Try to get that chest of drawers in the back bedroom, Em," Grandma yelled. "It has some things in it I'd like to save if you can. But you be careful."

I rushed back into the house to do what I could. The wind fanned the blaze and I would have to act fast. I went to the far end of the house, picked up the chest of drawers Clara had asked me to save and carried it out in one piece with a chest of silverware and a photograph on top, everything intact. I don't know how I did it, but something gave me superhuman strength. The second trip into the house proved useless; the fire, ashes, and pieces of partially burned articles had already broken through the ceiling, and flames were savagely licking the walls and furniture in the living room. I realized I *must* get out of that inferno. I gave up trying to save anything else.

My thoughts turned to my own little house and I carried water to pour on the grass between the two houses, but the flames were leaping across from the roof of the big house to the roof of the mobile home. My efforts were useless. Exhausted and out of breath, I had done all I could and went to the car to check on Grandma and Valerie. Clara was crying. This was the second time in her life she had lost everything to fire. Valerie was still sleeping soundly, oblivious to everything that happened.

Soon Grandpa and Ormie came home along with some neighbors who had seen the smoke and went to the field to tell them. But it was too late for them to help. Approximately thirty minutes from the time I discovered the roof on fire, everything was flattened to the ground. A pile of aluminum around the edge of where the mobile home stood told us where it used to be. The sod still stood there from the old house, but the contents were demolished. Twisted pieces from an old iron bed frame stuck up out of the ashes. The iron from the treadle sewing machine, pieces of silverware and other utensils showed up in the rubble, bent and charred. Everything burned up—all of our clothing, all the furniture and appliances, and all our photographs and keepsakes. We survived with only the clothing on their backs, the chest of drawers and its contents and the clean clothes still hanging on the clothesline. A lifetime of work and souvenirs for Grandma and Grandpa gone, Ormie's and my wedding presents along with souvenirs from our military service in World War II—all gone.   After the initial shock of the fire, we realized our good fortune in spite of the losses of our material possessions. We still had each other, and nobody in our family was killed or even burned. If this had happened in the middle of the night, possibly none of us would be here to tell the story. Life goes on, and although we will never forget that dreadful day, we realized we had a lot to be thankful for.

Living in the country brought many bonuses. Neighbors and friends are always willing to lend a helping hand in a time of need. People came from miles around, bringing clothing, bedding, and food to tide us over until we could get established again. The next morning, seven neighbors pulled into the field with tractors and drills to finish seeding the field with flax Ormie and Dode had started. Later the women in the community held showers for both Grandma and me to replace many household items.

Our sister-in-law Letha offered us a place to live until we could find suitable housing. We moved to her house for two weeks while we made other arrangements, or I should say our neighbors made arrangements for us. The landlord moved in a one-bedroom house for Grandma and Grandpa, and one of our good neighbors Alden Erickson moved in a sheep wagon for us to live in until we could get something better. At least we had a roof over our heads, even though the sheep wagon leaked. We had to move Valerie's baby buggy someone gave us so it wouldn't rain in on her. People gave us so many things, more clothing than we had before the fire. Our baby Valerie had lots of hand-me-down clothes and diapers.

The summer went by, and the harvesting was done. But another crisis hit us we didn't expect. Ormie came in from the field every night with his eyes swelled almost shut and had trouble breathing. We decided this ranching and farming couldn't be for us. Our little home was gone and he couldn't stand working in the grain, so we packed our stuff and moved back to Rapid City. Our good friends Ray and Esther Shepherd offered us a place to live with them until we could find a place of our own.

~CHAPTER 9~
OUR "STINKER" ARRIVES

Orman and I will never forget Ray and Esther's hospitality and friendship. We moved right in with them for two weeks until we bought our first house, not counting the small mobile home we lost in the fire on the ranch. We moved into our new home by the railroad tracks near Hwy. 79. We bought a bedroom set, a couch, an easy chair and a table and chair set. After this first of many moves, we settled in.

We moved in October of 1947, and in November we invited the Willey family for Thanksgiving. We celebrated Valerie's first birthday and spent Christmas there. But we ran out of water, and the contractor wouldn't make it good except for refunding our down payment. We found ourselves moving after living there only three months.

We fell in love with a two-story house in Caputa, a little town east of Rapid City. We rented it and loved living in a country setting. The house had two bedrooms upstairs with a bathroom between, just right for our little family: one bedroom for us and one for the two babies. Yes, two babies because I was pregnant again. The house had a living room, dining room and kitchen downstairs and a full basement. Our landlord lived across the street.

We loved the place in Caputa until spring when things began to happen. My brother Chris came to stay with us for a while, and he and Ormie went fishing for catfish on Rapid Creek in the evenings.

One night Chris, Valerie and I waited for Ormie to get home from work and I started preparing supper. I walked over to the refrigerator and something coiled around my feet. I let out a big screech and jumped about six feet into the air. I had stepped right in the middle of a big snake. Chris came to my rescue, grabbed a broom, dragged the snake away and killed it. I snatched Valerie off the floor where she was playing, and I never let her play on the floor again. I worried the baby I was carrying in my belly would be marked with a snake because I had heard the old wives tale that if something scared you while pregnant, your baby would be marked.

My niece Carol came to stay with us before I had my baby. She would take care of Valerie while I was in the hospital and help me awhile afterwards. On June 15, 1948, we headed to St. Johns Hospital where Valerie was born. I had labor pains almost as long as the first time. Alyce Marlene was born shortly after midnight on June 16, 1948. She weighed 7 lb. 3 oz. and she measured 21 inches long. When they gave her to me, I thought she looked exactly as Valerie looked when I first saw her; our second daughter was beautiful too. There's nothing quite as wonderful as seeing your new baby for the first time, to get acquainted after she kicked around inside you for so long. I couldn't wait to check her over to make sure she didn't have any markings of a snake. She was perfect, and as an experienced mother now, I thought I knew exactly what to do. Not so; each little person is different, and what works with one doesn't always work on the next one. Marlene was a good baby, probably because I didn't have time to fuss over her. My 18-month-old Valerie required a lot of attention, and sometimes I almost forgot I had Marlene until she cried to let me know she was hungry or needed changing. She is as precious to me today as she was then. Her daddy gave her a nickname, and to this day he calls her Stinker. We took her home from the hospital five days later wrapped up in a blanket, but I forgot it was summer and by the time we got home, she was speckled with heat rash.

"I can't live here with my babies anymore, honey," I said to Ormie. "I know those snakes are still in the basement and I'm afraid to let Valerie play on the floor and I can't put Marlene in the playpen."

"Don't worry," Ormie said, "I have plugged up any holes where they can get upstairs." But I had to do the laundry in the basement and that is where the blue racers were denned up in a pile of coal. I tried hard to forget about the snake that had coiled around my feet in the kitchen, but it kept nagging at me. One morning I rose up in bed to look out the window. I saw my husband carrying a big snake out toward the garbage.

Then something else happened. The landlord left on vacation and asked us to pick his strawberries while he was gone. Carol went across the street to pick them the next morning. "There's a man lying in the strawberry patch and he looks like he's dead!" Carol screamed. White as a ghost, she sat down in a kitchen chair and her bucket clattered to the floor. I called a neighbor lady who lived nearby. She investigated and found out it was the town drunk sleeping it off. The whole town knew him, but we hadn't heard about him. We watched from the window, and when he got up and left Carol went back over to pick the strawberries.

That wasn't the end of problems at our house in Caputa. One weekend, we took our little family and drove out to the ranch country to visit May and Cliff and Grandma and Grandpa. We were gone three days, and when we got back we unlocked the door of our house. Obviously someone had been in our house because we found a new vacuum cleaner set up in the living room.

"You and the girls stay right here," Ormie said, and he did a thorough search of the house, upstairs and down. We called the landlady and she said it probably was the last tenant who still had a key to our house. He had gotten drunk and thought he still lived there. He was a vacuum cleaner salesman. The landlady called him to come after his machine. Turned out he was the same man who was sleeping it off in the strawberry patch.

That was the last straw. Not knowing when the drunk would appear again or when one of those snakes would escape from the cellar, I didn't feel secure living there with my babies, and once more we looked for a new home. We found a little house in the Canyon Lake area in Rapid City; our landlord had remodeled his garage to make a small house, a kitchen/living room combined, a bathroom and one bedroom. But at that point, rentals were hard to find, and I would have lived anywhere except in the "snake house." We put Valerie's crib in the living room and Marlene's basket in our bedroom, and we made it our home while we looked for something larger.

We found an apartment next to my brother Richard and his family in Greenacres Apartments, which had been remodeled from an old motel. Our furniture got moved so often it's a wonder it lasted as long as it did. We enjoyed living next door to Richard and Arlene, who had Sharon and Wayne at that time. Later we found a house on Adams Street with two bedrooms, living room, bathroom and kitchen. It had only one drawback: the landlord lived upstairs and had to use our back door to go in and out. But we were comfortable there and had good neighbors who lived next door, Elmer and Bonnie Kanago, who had two boys, Jerry and Randy. We played cards and had coffee with them, and that summer Bonnie and I took all the kids to Canyon Lake where they could play in the water while we watched them.

We got our first little dog when we lived on Adams Street. He was a black cocker spaniel; he hadn't been trained yet, as he was just a few weeks old. Finally I had Marlene trained to sleep all night when we got Inky. Guess who had to get up in the middle of the night again to feed the little critter? But our little girls loved Inky so it was worth it.

The house on Adams Street had its disadvantages too. Our little girls woke up every morning with red spots all over their bodies, and I thought they must have chicken pox. I took them to see Dr. Owen. It didn't take him long to give me the diagnosis. "Those are bedbug bites," he said. He told us what to buy to fumigate with and we left for a few days to go to the ranch country. What next?

We moved again, this time to a little house on Maple Street. It also had two bedrooms and a bath. Once again we bettered ourselves by moving away from the bedbugs and the lack of privacy with the landlord living upstairs.

Settled again on Maple Street, we made a fishing trip to Wyoming and Yellowstone Park. We hitched a little trailer onto the back of our five-passenger Chrysler coupe and took off for a little vacation. We took the girls out to May and Cliff's, where we left them till we returned. We invited Chris and Carol to go with us. We packed food and bedding and camped out every night. Carol had a fold-up cot and the rest of us rolled our bedrolls out on the ground. We did quite a bit of fishing in every place Chris thought it looked "favorable," an expression we've never forgotten him using. We enjoyed Yellowstone Park and fished there too; we caught several messes to cook on our camp stove. We slept out under the stars, and one night had to sleep under a tarp to keep the rain from drenching us. A fun trip, even when a bear tried to get into our trailer as we moved along slowly. But Ormie stepped on the gas and we got away from him before he stole our food.

On our way home from Wyoming we picked up Valerie and Marlene at May and Cliff's. They had fun playing with their cousins Bonnie and Dennis out in the country, and we knew they had good care, but were happy to have our family back together again.

~Chapter 10~
Our "Butch" Arrives

I was pregnant again, this time due in November, during hunting season. Ormie got home from his hunting trip just in time to take me to the hospital. I got so front-heavy my hip went out when I tried to walk, quite painful. When Ormie arrived home he called Dr. Owen. "My wife can hardly walk," he said.

"Bring her to the hospital tomorrow morning and we will induce labor," the doctor instructed.

I was admitted and they proceeded to induce labor, first with castor oil in orange juice, which was to be followed with a shot. But the castor oil did the trick and the shots weren't necessary. I began to have contractions immediately and I called the nurse.

"You can't have that baby yet, the doctor isn't here yet," she said.

"You better get him here quick because I am going to have this baby soon," I said. "This is my third experience and I should know."

She took me to the delivery room and Doctor Owen got there just in the nick of time to deliver my baby.

"It's a boy," the doctor said. For some reason we thought it would be another girl, and couldn't believe we finally had our boy. Now we had to choose a boy's name and we settled on

Orman Ray. He was born on November 18, 1950, and weighed 8 lbs. ½ oz. A healthy baby boy, he had blond fuzzy hair and the nurses called him "cotton top." His Daddy passed out cigars to everyone he met when he told them we had a boy. He nicknamed his son Butch, and to this day he is Butch to our family. He adapted the use of his middle name Ray after he grew up. For several years we called him Ormie Ray to distinguish his name from his father's.

During my five days in the hospital, Ormie took the girls up to May and Cliff's to stay until I came home. Then Carol came again to help me awhile after we took our son home to meet his two sisters. Now we had our family, and were so proud of all three.

Valerie and Marlene, both under four, watched me give their new brother a bath and wanted to help with everything. One morning they both had their faces right there during the bathing process. When Butchie sprayed them with urine, they didn't come around much anymore at bath time.

We tired of moving around, but our family had grown and we needed more room. Ormie got acquainted with a realtor and we bought our second house about three years after the first one. It was on Elmhurst Drive in Canyon Lake, a cute little white house with an extra lot. Once again we moved, to stay this time. We planned to build a new house on the extra lot as soon as we could afford it. Grandpa and Grandma Willey came down to spend a few days. Grandpa helped Ormie build in some closets and chests of drawers upstairs for bedrooms for the kids. We kept Butch downstairs in our bedroom until he grew enough to go up and down stairs by himself.

Carol worked as a waitress in Rapid City after we brought Butch home, and there is where she met Chuck, whom she married. They moved their little trailer house into our yard, and Carol and June stayed in it while Chuck was gone overseas in the army. We met June's boyfriend Don, whom she married later. They all tell us to this day we taught them to play poker. We had many good times with those two couples.

Frances, Ann and Jean came to stay while Bill went to Denver to look for work. Frances worked and I took care of the girls and did their laundry, but Frances did all the ironing. It worked well for us all to live together for a while because Ormie had started working in the oil business and traveled, so I enjoyed having the company.

Valerie started kindergarten when we lived on Elmhurst Drive. It was just a short walk to school. I will never forget her first day there, and how I hated to leave her. I don't think she minded as much as I did.

One day in 1953, the phone rang and it was the realtor who had sold us our little house. He asked if he could bring some people out to look at the place. I was shocked because I didn't know Ormie had talked to him about selling our place, but sell it we did, lock, stock and barrel. All my furniture went, including my new automatic washing machine. Then my husband told me he had bought a brand new house, still under construction, and planned to buy all new furniture for it. I hated to give up my little house, and I gave him a little trouble when we closed the deal. From that time on, he always talked to me about any plans to buy or sell.

We rented a basement apartment while waiting for our new brick house on 44th Street. We went to California for Christmas. Ormie bought a new station wagon at the auction in Denver, and we invited his parents to go with us. We packed up the station wagon, Grandma and Grandpa in the second seat, the girls in the back and Butch in the front seat with us. We had a good trip and it turned out to be the first Willey reunion in Lancaster, California, at Noble and Marge's house. All five brothers and sisters and families came, and we had a fun time. We drove to Hollywood one day to do some sightseeing, and while walking down the street in Hollywood we ran into Pa Kettle. He grinned at us as we walked by. We went to the Phil Harris show too.

After we got home from California, our new brick house in South Canyon was ready to move into. We had two bedrooms upstairs and a den in the full basement. We put the kids all in one bedroom, and planned to put Butch downstairs when he got a little older. We bought all new furniture and I got my Wurlitzer piano.

Marlene started school while we lived in South Canyon. I wasn't so apprehensive about leaving her there the first day as I had been with Valerie because she had her older sister to walk with her to school and back every day.

We got the girls their first bicycle and Butch his riding tractor toy. They spent many hours learning to ride the bike, with a few skinned knees thrown in. Butch ran the little tractor around the yard for many miles.

After the girls left for school in the mornings, Butch had a lot of little guys to play with. He was only about four years old, and he had a few good buddies, Steve, Mike and Jeff. One morning he and Jeff got into a skunk while out playing. I knew it as soon as I saw him coming because I could smell him. I stripped him down outside and put him in the bathtub for a good scrub down, then put him down for a nap. Then I went outside, dug a hole and buried all his clothing. When I dug them up several months later, I put them in the laundry, and the odor was gone except when I ironed them.

Another time, I lost track of Butch, and I ran all over the neighborhood looking for him. I almost called the police to report him missing when I heard giggling in the basement. He and Jeff were hiding from me. Once, Butch's little friends blamed him for throwing rocks and breaking one of the neighbor's basement windows. It turned out the whole gang of little boys made a game out of seeing who could hit the window, and his rock happened to break it. It was a new housing development and so many kids lived there it was hard to determine who was actually the guilty party. We paid for the window, but I never knew for sure if our son did it or just got blamed for the deed.

Ormie bought two new cars, a red and white Ford station wagon and my 1954 Belair Chevy. It was turquoise and white, a 4-door sedan. We drove it to Oregon to visit relatives. It was the first time we ever left the kids with anyone overnight, and our vacation lasted three weeks. I didn't want to leave the kids with Grandma and Grandpa even though I knew they would take good care of them. We had a wonderful trip to Portland, Oregon, to visit Orman's sister Bonnie and Russ, aunts and uncles and cousins there. I vowed I would never leave my kids again for that long. Everything went fine, though, and I'm sure I suffered more than the kids did.

The following fall, Ormie went grouse hunting with some of his friends. They went north to Mud Butte, and then east to do their hunting. Sometime in the afternoon, my phone rang.

"Hello, is this Mrs. Willey?" a man's voice said.

"Yes it is," I answered.

"I am at the Rapid City Airport. We just had a call that your brother-in-law has been shot in a hunting accident. They are flying him in from Faith. Can you have someone at the airport to pick him up?" he asked.

"I will have someone there as soon as possible," I said. Now I knew there was a mix-up because I knew Aldy hadn't gone hunting with Ormie. I immediately put two and two together. This was my husband who was shot, not my brother-in-law.

I called Aldy, and he came to pick me up to go to the airport to pick up Ormie. I called Carol to stay with the kids until we got back. Aldy, a fast driver, made it to the airport in time to see the little plane come in with Ormie in it. He walked off the plane, but I don't think he should have because he looked pale and obviously in a lot of pain. We got him in the car and Aldy laid on the horn all the way to the hospital. He went to surgery immediately, and doctors removed several shotgun pellets from his back and arm, but many were left there. Ormie spent about a week there; they saved his arm, although it was doubtful at first, because most of the shotgun pellets had lodged in his left arm. He had nineteen of them in his back; they still show up in an x-ray. He felt fortunate to have survived that accident. He never had any bad feelings toward his friend who accidentally stumbled, making his gun go off, thus causing the accident. Bill and his wife Esther felt bad about it and couldn't do enough for us, and if my memory serves me correctly, they insisted on paying half of our hospital bill.

Living on 44th Street in our wonderful brick home didn't last long. So many young families lived there, and I found it very hard to handle. The kids had so many little friends, and I found it difficult to keep track of mine. I insisted they stay home to play; they always wanted to go to someone else's house. But I prevailed, and one morning after my two little girls left to walk to school, I was doing my breakfast dishes and looked out the kitchen window to check on Butch. He was four by this time and I counted 19 little boys out there playing with him. If he couldn't go play somewhere else, he invited all the kids to come play with him. Of course, if one wanted a drink, they all wanted a drink, and I began to realize I was the neighborhood babysitter.

We started looking for a place in the country.

1955 Marlene, Ormie Ray, Valerie

~Chapter 11~
The Boulder Canyon Years

We found our home in the country in Boulder Canyon halfway between Sturgis and Deadwood, South Dakota, in 1956. It was an old schoolhouse remodeled into a home many years before. Someone built a lean-to on each side of it; the west side addition had two bedrooms with a small bathroom between, and the east side addition had another small bedroom on one end, a porch dining room in the center and hookups for laundry in the other end near the back door. The bathroom was so small we joked about it being a left-handed bathroom, because your arm could barely reach around on the right of the stool to do the clean-up chores. It had a small shower and a sink, but no bathtub. A door opened into each bedroom. Once when May and Cliff visited us, I got up early one morning to get breakfast; half asleep, I rushed into the bathroom to wash my face.

"Good morning, Em," a voice startled me. Here was Cliff sitting on the stool giggling, and he said, "Sorry, I forgot to lock the other door." Quickly I ran out, leaving him to finish his chores.

Our rustic country house was equipped with a woodstove in the living room and a combination wood and electric stove in the kitchen. A large sink in one corner of the kitchen underneath a built-in cupboard was so low I almost had to stand on my head to wash dishes.

"If I were you I'd just get me an ax and chop that sink right out of there and then Orman will have to get you a new sink," my sister-in-law Gladys remarked the first time she came to visit. We solved that problem when Ormie and our neighbor Cliff built cupboards on two sides of the kitchen. I ended up with a brand new sink. I laid the new tile in the kitchen myself, and recovered our kitchen chairs. We moved the original door from the porch to a different place and built a cute little shadow box where the old door had been. I loved my little remodeled kitchen and now I even had a place for my pretty little knick-knacks and pictures.

Our pump house had an electric pump, which gave us water from the deep well. When we first moved there, I had my washing machine and rinse tubs there where I did my laundry and hung it all on the clotheslines to dry between the house and the pump house. We had a small barn with a fenced-in corral. Between the barn and the house was a playhouse someone built. The garage with log siding to match the siding on our house stood just outside the gate to the yard. It had only a dirt floor but was a good place to put the car in out of the weather. Tall jack pines surrounded the buildings, and just east of the house someone had put in seven hookups for house trailers. A couple of the spaces were occupied when we moved in, and we soon filled the other five.

Butch started first grade at Boulder Park School, which was just a short distance from the house, and he and the girls trudged off down the hill every day to attend the little one-room country school. Their teacher, Mayren Thomas, taught them and lived in the teacherage for most of the years we lived there. She lived for her schoolkids, and spent all her weekends making interesting lesson plans and projects for the kids to do in school. The girls graduated from the eighth grade in the county, but finally the little school closed and the kids were bussed into Sturgis. Butch started junior high in Sturgis, while the girls graduated from high school there.

The ten years we lived in Boulder Canyon were happy times for us, and it was a great place to raise our family. But we had some scary times there too. One day Valerie came in rubbing her eyes. The kids were out pulling weeds around the house because their Daddy promised them a penny for every weed they pulled. Big blisters stuck out of both of Valerie's eyes, so we rushed her to Sturgis to see the doctor. It turned out she was allergic to the weed killer Orman sprayed around the yard. She stayed in town with her Aunt Anna for a couple days until her eyes cleared up, and we were careful from that day on not to use that kind of spray to kill weeds.

Another time, Ormie came to the house carrying Marlene in his arms. For a few minutes she didn't respond, but finally opened her eyes. Daddy laid her on the couch for a while to make sure she was all right. The kids had been playing in the cattle chute and one of the other kids pushed her off. She landed on her back, knocking the wind out of her. It turned out she was fine, but it scared us.

The kids came home from school one day with a note from the county nurse who had been at school that day checking on the kids. The note said that Butch was very near-sighted and needed to have glasses right away because he couldn't see the blackboard from the front desk at school. We ended up making an appointment to have all the kids' eyes tested, and they all needed glasses, but Marlene only for reading. When Butch got his glasses, his personality changed from a shy little boy to much more outgoing kid. Now we knew why he always hung close to one of us when he was little.

Sometimes on the weekends we took the kids bowling, and in the winter we went ice skating. When they were little and we took them out to eat, the girls always liked to order shrimp, but Butch never failed to ask for a hamburger and fries. We enjoyed going to their school programs, especially at Christmas when they did their parts in the program. Their teacher was one-of-a-kind, always keeping them interested in their schoolwork.

As the years passed we sold some of our 140 acres, sold the property across the highway to a lawyer in Deadwood, and then developed the lots across the canyon to the south. Ormie rented a big dirt-moving outfit and built a road back to the property from the highway. We had the 40 acres surveyed and divided into lots and then started selling them. We named all the streets, and the main street is Willey Lane. Before we sold out, several people built homes there in the beautiful wooded acreage.

We couldn't make a good living at Boulder Park with our seven trailer spaces or even after we started taking in campers in the summer. Ormie had to find other work, and he had several jobs: he worked on the missile sites, worked at a filling station in Sturgis, and eventually went back to selling mutual funds and insurance.

Several experiences come to mind as I reminisce. Once on the way home from Sturgis, we came around one of the many bends in Boulder Canyon and one of the wheels came off our old Chevy. It rolled past us as the car came to a stop. Ormie was able to retrieve it and put it back on, and we made it home without any serious consequences. I remember several times sitting at home alone in a blizzard, waiting for the car to turn in our driveway with Ormie bringing my family home from school in a snowstorm. We had a blizzard once that snowed us in our house. The snow was piled three quarters of the way up on the door, and the drifts outside were higher than the house. But we shoveled our way out many of those storms. After the storm, the huge drifts challenged us to get through the snow to the barn and to school.

One morning right after Christmas I prepared breakfast while Ormie went out to do chores. I happened to look out my kitchen window and there saw my husband flying down the hill from the pump house on the new sled we had gotten the kids for Christmas.

"Who did we buy that sled for?" I asked Ormie when he came in from the barn with his milk pail brimming over.

"I guess partly for me; sure came in handy this morning," he said.

During the long winter months, I bought myself some learn-how books and taught myself new crochet stitches. I subscribed to the Reader's Digest Book Club, which gave me a lot of reading, but soon that wasn't enough for me. I subscribed to an art course and later a writing course, and although I didn't do much with either one of the courses then, they have been valuable to me in later years. I needed more than just keeping house, but we both believed I needed to be home with the kids. I had my schedule for housework: laundry on Monday, ironing on Tuesday, mending on Wednesday, baking on Thursday and every Friday I gave the house a thorough cleaning. We lived in Boulder Canyon ten years, until our kids grew up and attended high school.

~CHAPTER 12~
ANIMALS AT BOULDER PARK

Our family had a lot of animals when we lived at Boulder Park. We named our first dog Boots because he had white legs that matched the white stripe down his nose. Ormie trained him to go after the paper and to bring the milk cow to the barn from the pasture every night.

"Go get the paper, Boots," or, "Go get the cows," Ormie commanded, and off he went to do his job. A smart dog, but Boots wasn't smart enough to stay off the highway, and one night a truck ran over him and killed him.

We replaced Boots with Honey, a little honey-colored pooch who eventually suffered the same fate. Then in 1958 Carol and Chuck brought the kids a Christmas present, a furry, cuddly little puppy named Hindsdale Tiny Tim. He was a thoroughbred Norwegian elkhound, the runt of the litter belonging to Gertrice and Alfred Hinds, who raised them. I wasn't too happy about getting another dog; I didn't like to hear the kids cry about their lost pets. But Timmy was there with a red ribbon around his neck, and so cute we all fell in love with him. Timmy was a good dog and protective of the kids. Ormie built him a house out in the yard, which he slept in every night. He ran for his doghouse once during an electrical storm, but when lightning struck his house, he vacated and never went back in there again, but slept on our first step instead. Often I went out the door to find two cats lying on top of him, taking advantage of his warm coat of fur. Timmy stayed with us through the move to Rapid City and then traveled with us to Grand Junction, Colorado, when we moved there in 1967. Butch took him up on the mountain at Mesa, Colorado, where he lived in 1973 but finally had to put him down. Timmy was our last pet and we missed him. Butch was in the second grade when we got him and he lived several years after Butch graduated from high school.

We bought two saddle horses. One was Princess, a white pony so gentle the kids could ride her, go under her or anything they wanted to. The kids spent many hours with Princess, taking turns riding her. Brownie was our other horse, a more aggressive horse, and he ran Princess off a bank of the canyon and broke her leg. We had to get rid of her, another big disappointment for the kids. We finally sold Brownie too, because he was too frisky for the kids.

The cats? We had plenty of them. One day we counted 19 of them running around the place and decided it was time to reduce the number.

"We have to have some of the cats put to sleep," we told the kids at breakfast one morning, "but you can pick out two to keep."

"Why can't we have one cat in the house?" Marlene asked.

"Yes," I said, "you can have one in the house but you will have to take care of it and clean up any messes it makes." She agreed and they told us which two cats they wanted to keep. So that day after the kids left for school, we did the job. We turned a laundry tub upside-down and put chloroform under it. Then we started catching cats, and one by one we put them under the tub. In the process we almost killed one of the neighbor's cats, but rescued it in time to save it. We told the kids a little white lie; they didn't know we did the job ourselves.

We purchased a couple of milk cows, so twice a day one of us had to milk the cows and separate the cream from the milk. We bought an old-fashioned cream separator and a churn, made our own butter and had plenty of milk and cream.

Once we bought a steer calf to raise for beef. The calf became a pet and we all played with him so much he playfully tossed his head around and tried to butt us. The bad part was the calf was still playful after he grew up, and one day he cornered me in the barn and butted me around like a plaything. I didn't have any broken bones but had black and blue marks for weeks. I didn't mind at all when Ormie decided to slaughter that steer for beef.

We raised chickens too. We bought a hundred baby chicks, made a makeshift little coop for them and managed to raise most of them in spite of the poor facilities. They had free run of the place and often walked up on the porches of our renters. In the fall we butchered them and canned them. Along with raising chickens, we also purchased some laying hens; they supplied us well with fresh eggs.

We had no machinery, and not much money, but we were determined to make our little place in the country work for us. We spaded up a large garden with an old-fashioned spade and a lot of elbow grease. Our plan was to raise enough vegetables so I could can the surplus for winter use. We planted long rows of everything from lettuce and radishes to turnips and green beans. We set out dozens of tomato and cabbage plants. Finally the seeds sprouted and we waited for our first taste of fresh vegetables. We had delicious sweet peas, tender green lettuce and plump red radishes. The string beans would be ready in a few weeks. The tomato plants were blooming profusely, promising us big red tomatoes later in the summer. Our garden was out in the corral where there was plenty of fertilizer in place. We were feeling quite smug about our success as gardeners when one night dark clouds came up and a hailstorm wiped out everything. All our hard work was beat into the ground and we had to plant it over again.

When we bought our place in the country, we had dreams of having our own animals, our own milk, butter and cheese, our own beef, our own chickens and a big garden to help feed our family. For the most part, our dreams came true and we survived happily there for ten years. We realized how many hardships our parents had gone through years before, and we had a lot to learn the hard way, just as they did.

~Chapter 13~
More Memories of Boulder Park

The Lawrence County sheriff appeared at our door one day. "Your family will have to evacuate. The fire is headed this way," he said. A big forest fire around Deadwood threatened our home.

"Each of you pack a couple changes of clothes and pick one favorite toy to take with you and get in the car," I told my kids. We had to move quickly. Ormie was gone on his sales job. I hesitated a moment, trying to think what important things I should save. I went to the file cabinet and picked out some important papers and packed some precious family pictures. I took my new Singer sewing machine with me, the one I bought with money from my dad's estate. When I got out to the car, the kids were already there with our dog Timmy and two cats. I hadn't even thought of the animals. I drove down to the teacherage where our teacher Miss Thomas lived to pick her up because she didn't have a car and I knew she would need a ride.

"We don't have to leave now," Miss Thomas said. "I just heard on the radio the wind switched and the fire is going the other way." The authorities had cancelled the evacuation and we went back home. However, we left the car loaded for a day or two, until the fire was under control.

The first summer we lived in Boulder Canyon, tourists stopped in now and then to ask if they could camp under our trees. Our place was in the northern part of the Black Hills, only seven miles from historic Deadwood and another mile from Lead, home of the famous Homestake Gold Mine. It was also a short drive to Mount Rushmore, the Passion Play in Spearfish, Custer State Park where the buffalo roamed freely, and other tourist attractions in the Black Hills. Restroom facilities weren't adequate for campers, but we let them stay for a dollar a night with the stipulation they take their own trash with them when they left. Soon we had many campers in our beautiful park but got tired of cleaning up after them. We built a wash house behind the trailer court with restrooms for men and ladies and enough space for our washing machine and rinse tubs. Finally I had a better place to do our laundry, and it was much handier for our permanent renters to do their laundry. We went into the camping business in earnest and named our campground Boulder Park Trailer Court & Campground. Every summer our park filled with tents and recreational vehicles of all types. It provided a little extra income in the summer, but when school started in the fall, the tourist season ended.

In 1964 we moved to Sturgis so the kids would be closer to high school. We rented an old house on Davenport Street, a two-story with a full basement. We rented our house in Boulder Canyon to a young married couple, Alva and Irene Roberdeau. They took care of our small business there, collected the rent for us and kept up the place. In the spring we moved back home and in 1965 decided to build a store onto the house so we could accommodate our growing crowd of campers with groceries.

My brother Chris came to help build the store while his wife Kathy and I drove to Kentucky for her father's funeral. I enjoyed visiting my sister Ruth, her husband Tob and their daughter Adele Lee, who lived in Kentucky. I left my kids home to take care of the house and the campground. When I returned home, Ormie and Chris had finished the store and even put new siding on the house to match the store. Then we had a painting bee. Some of our friends and relatives came and the whole building got a paint job in red. I cooked for the crew and it turned out to be a fun day. We stocked the new store with staple foods, got a good deal on a big refrigerator display case and we were in business. It was nice to finally have an office to work out of for the campers, and we developed a good summer business.

We had a lot of company when we lived at Boulder Park. Whenever anyone came to the Black Hills from the ranch country north of us, they stopped in. And many times on Sunday friends drove up from Rapid City or over from Spearfish to visit. My weekends were almost always busy, making sure my house was clean and having something baked to serve to company. I often said if I didn't want to cook on Sunday we had to get up early and leave. But we enjoyed having company, and as I look back on it, I enjoyed the cooking and baking too.

I went to bed one night with a slight sore throat and when I woke up the next morning, I couldn't swallow. I had a fever and Ormie took me to the doctor. He took my temperature, examined my throat and sent me straight to the hospital. In the middle of the night, something pulled me toward a bright, shimmering light. It was at the end of a very long black tunnel. The tunnel got smaller and very narrow. The light got brighter as I got closer to it. The rays lit up the entire tunnel, reaching out to me, enticing me in, and I wanted to go.

"I can't go yet. I have to raise my kids, and I can't leave Ormie," I said to myself. I forced myself to resist the strong force that was pulling at me and I woke up. Questions raced through my mind. What was this force that was tugging at me? Was this God trying to get me to Heaven and I convinced Him I had to finish raising my kids first? Later my sister Anna, who worked at the hospital and was on duty that night, told me I had a temperature of 105 that night and they didn't know if I would survive.

"I'm going home now, but if she gets any worse, call me and I'll call Ormie," I heard Anna saying to someone. Now many years later, I remember the night as if it were yesterday. Was I dreaming? Hallucinating? Is this what really happens when we die? If this was real—and I believe it was—then death will be an easy, pleasant experience. I wanted to follow the light in the worst way, but my children and husband took priority.

After ten years, the girls were both in Rapid City—Valerie in business school and Marlene at the School of Mines. Ormie got involved working for Hamilton Funds, Inc., selling mutual funds and insurance. I even got licensed for the job, but when I ran out of relatives to sell to, I gave it up, especially when I walked down the street one day to service clients' accounts. A dog barked at me and acted like he would eat me alive. I turned around, went back home, threw my briefcase on the table and announced, "This job isn't for me."

Ormie was one of the top salesmen in the division, and won a trip to Las Vegas for both of us. We drove there and were given one of the suites to stay in, and we learned the ways of Las Vegas and gambling in between his sales meetings. On the long trip home, we had a lot of time to talk. It was getting harder to run the campground without the help of our girls. They no longer lived at home, and Ormie traveled a lot for his job, so that left only Butch and me to run the campground. He was a big help; he did all the mowing, raking and other things. But I knew he would be leaving home too before long. On the way home from Las Vegas in 1966 we decided to put our place up for sale. After ten years of living in our happy Boulder Canyon home, we would sell out and move to Rapid City, where Ormie could devote himself fully to his sales and I would be able to find work somewhere. When we got home we put the wheels in motion for an auction.

Cliff and May came and boxed up all the stuff in the store,

and we spent several days packing things in boxes that we wanted to keep and sorting out things to discard. We hired Francis Haley, the local auctioneer, and he did a great job of getting rid of every last thing we owned except what we decided to keep. On October 17, 1966, we had our auction. The place was sold to Hannah and Allen Oedekoven, my niece and her husband. We loaded up all our personal possessions and went to Rapid City where we stayed in a motel until we found our house. We found it hard to leave our happy little home where our kids grew up. We realized they would soon all be grown up and leaving home. When we drove away, with a lump in my throat and a tear in my eye I looked back at the old house and waved a fond farewell.

1963 Ormie Ray, Mom, Valerie, Dad, Marlene

~CHAPTER 14~
BACK TO RAPID CITY, TWO WEDDINGS AND A BABY

Valerie came home one weekend and announced that she and her boyfriend Marlyn Stubbe planned on getting married. Marlyn was a student at the School of Mines, and he wasn't exactly a stranger because he had been to our house in Boulder Canyon several times when he came to pick Val up. It didn't surprise us, but with both of them only 19, they seemed too young. We could see their determination to get married, and between moves we managed to arrange for the wedding. My good friend Esther Goerndt offered to bake the cake and have the reception at her house. Then we went shopping for a wedding dress because I didn't have the time to make one; besides, my sewing stuff was still packed. Marlyn's parents came for the wedding from their home in DeSmet, South Dakota. It was held at the Baptist church in Rapid City. Orman proudly walked Valerie down the aisle to give her away even though he had some misgivings about her getting married so young. The newlyweds left for a short honeymoon in the Black Hills before they returned to their small apartment near the School of Mines. Valerie worked in the office at a dairy near there.

We found our new home in South Canyon west of town, a three-bedroom tri-level. We bought new furniture because all our old stuff sold at the auction. We moved in and got settled, with Marlene in her bedroom across the hall from ours and Butch in his bedroom on the lower level.

Ormie traveled a lot selling Hamilton Funds and insurance, Butch was a junior in high school and Marlene attended the School of Mines.

As for me, I was at loose ends, so I started looking for a job. I hadn't worked since I got out of the army and I didn't want to work in the food business as I had done that. I was no longer qualified to teach school without going back to college. I saw an ad in the paper for learning machine embroidery at a place called Masters Awards. Because it was within walking distance of the house, I applied for the job. They hired me and it took me at least a month to learn how to do the embroidery, but finally with a lot of patience from my boss I mastered the job. He paid me the minimum wage of $1.40 an hour to sit there and practice. I embroidered a lot of shirts and other things and even designed my own patterns to put on them. I loved the job, and before long I got my first promotion.

By then Marlene had a steady boyfriend. She met Norm Johnson at the School of Mines, and it wasn't long before they announced their engagement and planned a June wedding. This time I had the time and was settled enough to make Marlene's wedding dress and one for Valerie, who would be the maid of honor. Marlene chose a simple pattern and we went shopping for material. She chose yellow and white for her colors; the bride's dress was white and Valerie's yellow. I borrowed Esther's cake pans and made the cake myself this time. Norm's parents, brother and sister and their families came from Parker, South Dakota, for the wedding; it was held at the same church where Valerie and Marlyn tied the knot. Most of the people we invited came to the reception at our house. I picked yellow roses and white daisies from our flowers in the back yard. The bride and groom opened their gifts in our backyard before they left on their honeymoon. They spent the first night of their honeymoon at Custer State

Park in the Black Hills and then went on to Richland, Washington, where Norm landed his first job after graduating from the School of Mines.

Within a year both of our daughters were married and no longer living at home. We had only our son left at home, and Butch stayed with us until he graduated from high school.

One day our son-in-law Marlyn interrupted my housework when he showed up at the door. "Can you come? Valerie wants you; she is having pains," Marlyn said when I answered the doorbell. It was the morning of March 28, 1967. I grabbed my coat and went with him. I was quite sure Valerie's pains must be labor pains.

"You better call the doctor," I said to Marlyn. "He may want her to come to the hospital." Sure enough, the doctor told him to bring Valerie to the emergency room.

"I'm going to have the baby today," Valerie said as she came out of the doctor's office looking a little afraid but happy. She entered the hospital, I finally contacted Ormie, and he, Marlyn and I waited for the baby to come. The nurse brought her out to show us—a beautiful baby girl. They named her Jennie Lynn.

We now had our first grandchild, and that summer when Marlyn went to basic training in Washington State for six weeks, I got to take care of Jennie in the daytime while Val worked. I enjoyed giving her a bath every morning. Proud to be grandparents for the first time, Ormie and I both had fun playing with her.

It would be hard to move away, but we soon found out we would be moving again.

"Can you be in Grand Junction, Colorado, by January first?" It was the voice of Jerry Flaherty, Ormie's regional manager in Denver. "The company will pay for the move," he said. We had seen Jerry many times at regional sales meetings. The new job of division manager was to begin in 1968, and Ormie would take over the western slope of Colorado, everything west of the Rocky Mountains. Even though we had only been in our house for a year, we couldn't pass up the opportunity. I hated to give up my job at Masters Awards because I was getting good at machine embroidery.

We called the moving company and planned our move for Christmas afternoon. We had dinner with Aldy and Margo and took off right after dinner. Butch drove the old pickup and Ormie our Pontiac. It was cold and snowy, and the prospect of driving through windy Wyoming worried me a little. We made it to Lusk, Wyoming, that night and stayed in a motel. Butch had our dog Timmy with him in the pickup and we left him in the truck to sleep.

The next morning it was 25 degrees below zero, but Timmy survived just fine. We started west again toward Casper and Rawlins. We made it to Rawlins, Wyoming, but traveled through a blizzard most of the way. At times we could barely see Butch in the truck ahead. We decided that night we would take Timmy in the motel with us because it was still snowing, blowing and very cold. It was warm in the motel and he huffed and puffed all night because he wasn't used to sleeping in a warm place with his heavy winter coat.

The next morning, the sun was out, the storm appeared to be over and we started on the last lap of our trip to our new home. The roads were still snow-packed, but the snow plows had been through and we had much better traveling that day. We arrived in Grand Junction about noon and checked into the Bar X Motel on North Avenue, a place the company provided for us until we could find a house. We stayed there two weeks while we did our house hunting.

~Chapter 15~
At Home in Grand Junction

Butch enrolled in high school as a junior, and we found our house to rent on Mesa Avenue, a four-bedroom. One bedroom was in front of the house next to the front door, a perfect place for our office. The moving van delivered our household stuff, we settled in and Ormie went to work as division manager. We held monthly meetings at various motels, and Ormie began to motivate the representatives who were already there and to hire new ones. We enjoyed the work; it was an exciting time for us. I did the bookwork and arranged for lunches to serve at the meetings. In one year we were successful in doubling the sales force and doubling the sales.

Ormie and Butch got involved in hunting in western Colorado and went on several elk hunting trips. We loved the fishing there at many lakes where we caught trout, but our favorite pastime was to grab our fishing poles, a sandwich and a couple cans of beer and head for either the Colorado River, Gunnison River or a canal close by to go fishing for catfish. Where the Gunnison River flowed into the Colorado was the best spot. We bought a small camp trailer and went on weekend camping trips.

We joined a square dancing class, which involved several short trips for square dance rallies. We met Valerie and Marlyn in Snowmass, Colorado, once for a rally there because they were heavily into square dancing too after they moved to Denver. It was so much fun, and we met some of our lifelong friends at square dance classes, especially Ted and Sharon Saunders. They were young enough to be our kids but we had a lot in common.

In 1968, we hosted the first Willey family reunion since 1953. We held it on Grand Mesa where we rented a couple cabins, and I did all the cooking, most of it ahead of time. We had a good turnout and it was a fun time. Relatives came from South Dakota, California and Oregon. We had hot weather in Grand Junction in the summer but up on the mountain it wasn't so bad. One evening a bunch of us drove down the mountain to attend a dance at the Moose Club where we all had a great time.

On March 23, 1970, we got a phone call from Ft. Leonard Wood, Missouri. It was Val telling us she gave birth to our first grandson, Todd Marlyn Stubbe. We welcomed him but didn't get to see him until he was nine months old when they came for a visit.

On September 14, 1970, Marlene called to tell us about her first-born and our second grandson, Eric Norman Johnson. They all came to visit us in our trailer when Eric was only three months old. Jennie was three by then and she entertained us all with her singing. Little Eric was fussy because he had a bad cold, I think. Todd made some nine-month baby noises and we got them all on tape.

Life in Colorado was great; it was the first time we had ever lived outside of South Dakota since we got out of the army except for the six months in Ft. Peck, Montana. But politics got in the way, and one of the vice presidents in the company wanted our division and we got shoved out. We could have stayed in a lesser position but opted to bow out for good even though we had been loyal to that company for years. A situation we had no control over told us we had to move on to something new.

Ormie tried sales jobs at different things; he sold furniture and John Deere industrial equipment, and worked as a credit manager in a department store. Our income decreased when we lost the division, and I found a job at a lumber company that wanted an older person they could train their way, and I took the plunge. I applied and got the job. I learned to operate an adding machine first and then the posting machine, and for the first time in my life I was a machine bookkeeper, a job I had always wanted to do from high school on. I liked the work, but the working conditions didn't suit me, and after a year I moved to St. Mary's Hospital to do the same kind of work for more pay. I liked it there until they put in teletype machines, and I had a new supervisor who was more interested in sitting around talking to all the men employees than working with me. Finally I gave my notice and I was out of a job. In the meantime, Orm had started his job with the John Deere Company and was making good money.

We moved from the four-bedroom house when we bought a new 12- by 65-foot Geer mobile home. We had our own home instead of throwing rent money out the window. It had two bedrooms, one of which Butch occupied until he moved out on his own. We lived there about six years. We all worked, Orm at his various selling jobs, me at my two bookkeeping jobs and Butch as a drug wholesale distributor.

During those years in the Geer mobile home we met our long-time good friend Bonnie Jayne, who has since divorced and married again to Jack Payne, and the two of them have been our friends ever since.

In the fall of 1973 we had three deaths in the family. Ormie's brother Aldy, my brother Richard and May's husband Cliff all passed away that fall. All three were only in their 50s. We made a trip to Rapid City for Aldy's funeral, taking Valerie with us from Denver. After we got back, I went hunting with Ormie up to the Raggedy Mountains on Rudy and Mary Volks' place. I slipped on a rock and fell, breaking two ribs. It was a three-mile walk back to where our camper was parked at the ranch, and then the two-hour ride home — a painful experience.

Not long after that, Cliff passed away, and again we went to Denver, picked up Valerie and went to Lemmon. Cliff died in a tragic fire that took him and their home. While there, we helped May go through the ashes and what was left to retrieve a few charred pictures or whatever she wanted to try to save or redo. We didn't go to Sunnyside, Washington, for my brother Richard's funeral. Three people very close to us were laid to rest in the fall of 1973. But life goes on.

We found a good buy on 23rd Street, a fixer-upper house that we bought for $9,000. We put our trailer house up for sale and found a buyer. We moved into the house, put in new carpeting and drapes, cleaned it up and sold it six months later for a profit of $6,000. In the meantime we had bought our camper and lived in it while we were house hunting. We stored all our furniture at a moving company, and decided it was a good time to take a trip.

I called my sister May, she flew to Grand Junction and we all went to Kentucky to visit our sister and brother, Ruth and Bill, who came from Virginia to see us. In the summer of 1974 we had a good trip to Kentucky in our new-to-us car, a two-door Oldsmobile. We stopped along the highway at roadside parks to eat our lunches and suppers and had breakfast in restaurants. We did a lot of sight seeing on that trip, both going and coming back. Some of those stops were the Eisenhauer Memorial in Abilene, Kansas, and the Abraham Lincoln Memorial near Hodgeville, Kentucky. There is a replica of the small log house where Lincoln was born. Best of all, we enjoyed a whole day at Opryland in Nashville, Tennessee.

When we returned from the trip we found our house on Thompson Road in Orchard Mesa. It was a red three-bedroom ranch-style with a large yard and a wonderful garden spot. We raised the best vegetables there we ever had, sweet corn, beautiful beefsteak tomatoes and a lot of other things.

By this time Ormie had landed a job as division manager for another investment company and had a furnished office downtown. I needed something to do, and I remembered my machine embroidery experience from Rapid City. One day I saw an ad in the paper for an embroidery machine. We went to look at it and I bought it. It took me awhile to get into it again, but when I did I put an ad in the paper, and before long I had all the work I wanted, doing embroidery on bowling shirts, business shirts, etc. I loved it, and was able to bring in a few dollars in the process.

Butch graduated from high school in Grand Junction. Before that he worked at a printing shop after school and on Saturdays. He wasn't afraid of work and always had a job. After graduation he held down a job at a drug company for several years. For a while he moved to Colorado Springs with a friend and they worked there. Right after graduation he started college at the community college, but after one quarter he came home and threw his books on the table.

"Dad and Mom, you are wasting your money sending me to college. I want to work for a while and maybe I'll go back later." We respected his honesty and his right to work at a job instead. He never got a degree, but he learned through the school of hard knocks to be a darn good plumber. He did take some classes in Washington, and today he has his own thriving plumbing business. We are proud of him for making it on his own without a lot of college.

During the nine years in western Colorado, our girls and their families came to visit several times, and we went to see them, Val and Marlyn in Denver and Marlene and Norm in Anaheim. We attended a Willey reunion in 1971 in Prairie City, South Dakota, at Grandma Willey's house, and another one in 1973 at Ramona, California, at Gladys and Jack's house. Those were good years in Colorado in spite of the setbacks in Ormie's career. We enjoyed the climate: very little snow in the winter and none of the electrical storms in the summer we had experienced in South Dakota.

While living in Grand Junction we went on several convention trips via the various mutual fund and insurance companies Ormie worked for, to New Orleans, Cedar Rapids, Denver and Portland, Oregon. We made several trips back to South Dakota to keep track of the lots we still owned in Boulder Canyon, and twice in the fall of 1973 for funerals.

On October 8, 1974, we had another addition to our family. Marlene and Norm had their second son, Ryan Scott Johnson. They lived in Anaheim, California, then so we didn't get to see Ryan until they came for a visit the next summer. He called me Grandmama when he first started talking. Ryan was instrumental in getting me to stop smoking when he said to me once, "You shouldn't smoke, Grandma."

In 1976, we were 56 and 59. We couldn't draw social security yet, but we did have some savings, and due to losing our three brothers, we decided not to wait for retirement age. We would do some traveling and work enough along the way to keep our savings intact. We sold out lock, stock and barrel. We bought a 24-foot trailer, hooked it onto our 1970 Ford pickup and hit the road. We would be highway hobos, desert rats, or whatever you wanted to call us. We would be free to do what we wanted and see some of our beautiful country while we were still young enough to enjoy it. We listed the place with a realtor, and before long we hit the road to let our wheels take us where they wanted to go.

~Chapter 16~
We Retire the First Time

We listed our place with a realtor on May 6, closed on June 3, and a month later on July 6, 1976, we found ourselves on the road headed for Lancaster, California. The first lap of our journey would last for more than a year. Butch had moved away from home permanently by then. We sold our home and everything in it except what we could load into our pickup and travel trailer. The Lord willing, we set out to see all fifty states.

We pulled out of Grand Junction about 4:00 p.m. and stopped in Green River, Utah, for a cocktail, steak and salad. We started out again about 8:00 even though it was still hot out there. We had to stop several times to let old Henry (our Ford pickup) cool off. We added water after it boiled over.

"No more driving in the heat," we told ourselves. We decided to drive all night until it started getting hot, then stop somewhere and plug Poopsie (our trailer) in and get some sleep.

We talked to some people on the CB as we traveled along. Orm's handle was Rolling Stone and mine was Tagalong. We found the CB a handy thing to have in our rig, to help locate things in a city before we got there if we needed to. We drove all night to beat the heat and stayed at Beaver, Utah, in a KOA camp where we could plug in and get some relief from the heat with our air conditioner. Actually it was 8:00 in the morning when we got to Beaver and we stayed there all day, catching up on sleep, getting cooled off and getting our laundry done.

At 8:00 p.m. that night we took off again thinking it would be cool to drive, but when we drove through Las Vegas at 2:30 a.m., it was 102 degrees. There went our decision for driving at night to beat the heat. We pulled into the little town of Jean just west of Las Vegas and slept a couple hours before we headed out again for Lancaster at 4:00 a.m. Our truck heated and cut out on us many times, and we began to think we would have to be towed in. But we limped along and finally got to Barstow to a truck stop where we had a good breakfast before we limped into Lancaster, very hot and tired.

We lived in Lancaster for nine days, parked next door to Orm's brother Noble and Marge. We had meals together, went to garage sales with them, played poker and caught up on a lot of visiting. We had a nice little patio, lawn, trees and all the comforts of home. *This IS our home*, I wrote in my diary. *How quickly we changed our lifestyle, and so far we love it, in spite of the troubles we had with old Henry.*

July 15 we got up at 4:30 to take Grandma to the Los Angeles airport to catch her plane to Modesto, California, where she would visit Orman's sister Gladys and Jack for a while. We had breakfast at Sambo's on the way and saw Grandma off on her flight, then drove back to Lancaster.

The next two days Orm worked on old Henry to try to get it running right. On July 18, Noble, Marge, Orm and I got in Zam (their car) and went to Las Vegas and stayed downtown at Binions Horseshoe, playing slots and blackjack all the next day. We saw a show at the Las Vegas Plaza, Reuben Huber's band from Bison, South Dakota. We had a ball and headed back to Lancaster the next day.

We got Henry packed with clothes and some lunch and got ready to head out for San Jose to see Marlene and Norm on July 22. We stopped by the ocean near Monterey and ate our lunch off the back of the truck, then took a walk along the beach and arrived at San Jose about 6:30.

We relaxed the next day, visiting with Marlene, Eric and Ryan. Eric was almost six by then and Ryan almost two, and it was fun to see how they had grown. Norm took us to San Francisco one day. We took along a lunch and had a picnic in the park, rode the trolley to downtown, and walked around the financial district and Chinatown. We had a fun day. Next day Norm took us on a mountain ride in the evening. The nights there are nice and cool, and it's not too hot in the daytime. The next night we went to a beautiful Mexican restaurant. On the way home we had to stop and get some milk for Ryan because he was crying after being such a good little kid all through dinner; he got hungry all of a sudden.

We had a relaxing visit and on July 27 we headed out for Modesto to visit Gladys and Jack and Grandma. It was very hot and we didn't want to use the air conditioner, but Henry made it without a hitch. We sat around the table visiting until after midnight. The next afternoon we drove to Fresno to visit Jerry and Nancy. We had a delicious dinner and a good visit there.

We left early the next morning to go home to our Poopsie in Lancaster, and enjoyed seeing all the fruit orchards on the way. We traveled 828 miles, but were glad to be home in Lancaster again. *Home is wherever we want it to be and it's a good feeling*, my diary says.

While in Lancaster we made several trips to China Lake to watch Roland and Richie play in Little League baseball, and enjoyed it a lot. We went with Noble and Marge to Green Valley where Marge bought chicken dinners. We played poker almost every night, and enjoyed visits from their kids off and on, Dolyce and Bob and Boys, Beebe and Laura and Bryan and Larry, Debbie and their kids. I kept Poopsie cleaned up and did laundry right across the street at the laundry room. We had many suppers together and a family garage sale at

Dolyce and Bob's one weekend. Orm worked on Henry quite a bit, hoping we could get it running without heating when we got ready to leave.

On August 11, we got our 10-day fishing licenses for $10 apiece. We got liver and night crawlers for bait, and fixed a lunch to take along to Quail Lake where I caught one striped bass. We went to Pyramid Lake and came home via Lake Hughes, then stopped at Apollo Park in Lancaster and fished a little longer. We got home before dark and I paid dearly for our fishing trip with a bad case of sunburn. *I don't know if that one fish was worth it,* I wrote. August 14 we tried to go fishing at the Aqueduct but it was too windy. We drove back through Little Rock and bought some fresh cucumbers, peaches, tomatoes, cantaloupe and sweet corn. The next day we went to the Aqueduct again and Orm caught a 15-inch striped bass before the wind got the best of us again. The next day we went to Apollo Lake to fish and Orm caught one trout before the wind came up. August 18, he finally caught a nice catfish out of the Aqueduct. August 20 was the last day for our fishing license. *I got skunked again and Orm caught another 5-pounder and a small one. We went to bed early pooped from our long fishing period,* my diary states.

We had the neighbors over the next day for a fish fry and some peach cobbler. August 23, Orm's birthday, we went to the Moose Club in the evening, had a birthday drink and went to a Japanese restaurant for supper.

For the next five days we had fun with the neighbors, played poker, and ate at each other's places. I worked on my state flower quilt and did laundry. Then on Saturday night we all went to the Moose Club for supper and danced until 11:30. The next day we relaxed and talked about moving on soon.

Marlene, Norm and boys arrived for a visit on Sunday, September 5. I fixed chicken and potato salad, tomatoes and cookies for supper. Eric slept on our couch; the rest stayed over at Noble and Marge's. They left the next day after lunch, after an enjoyable short visit.

"Wouldn't it be easier to poke a hole in the son of a bitch?" Noble yelled as he poked his head out the kitchen window when he saw Orm dipping water out of our sagging awning. We woke up that morning to a heavy rain, and the water was so heavy it bent the pole it rolled up into and we had to buy a new one — one more lesson learned about RV traveling.

One day Bill and Frances called and we made plans to meet them in Las Vegas on September 20, then go on to Colorado, South Dakota and points south for the winter.

September 19 — my 56th birthday — I got cards from everyone. My sweetie took me out for breakfast at Rose Marie's and then stopped at the Willey garage sale for a little while at Bob and Dolyce's.

We enjoyed our stay in Lancaster with Noble and Marge and their family and our couple of nice visits with Marlene and family, but we got itchy feet and decided to hit the road again.

1989 On the Road

~Chapter 17~
On the Road Again

September 21, 1976, we pulled out of Lancaster early, excited about getting on the road again. Poor old Henry heated up again going over the Baker Hill, so we stopped at a rest area awhile to let it cool off. Then we pulled into the Golden Manor in Las Vegas, where we had agreed to meet Bill and Frances. We got the trailer set up and decided to check out a few casinos — Sy's and Silver City — then had supper at the Stardust Palm Room. We got back to Poopsie at 2:00 a.m.

Bill and Frances arrived the next afternoon and we gabbed and ate supper before we went downtown to play the slots. We didn't get to bed till 3:00 a.m. We slept in the next morning and went over to their RV for bacon and eggs. It rained, so the four of us played poker in the trailer awhile before we went to town to play; we got home in the wee hours again. We had breakfast in our RV the next morning and then went to Honest Johns and other casinos; we lost more money before we came home to cook supper and visit till bedtime.

After visiting and having a great time with Bill and Frances for two days and nights, we decided to say goodbye and head out for Colorado. We left early on September 24 and got as far as Salina, Utah, where we camped at the same place we did on July 6 on our way to California.

September 26, Grand Junction, here we come! my diary says.

We arrived at Butch's place in Fruita, Colorado, about 1:00. We met Katie and liked her very much. She cooked a wonderful dinner—crown roast of pork, peas, salad and pie. We went to bed early, tired from our trip. We spent three days there in Fruita and Grand Junction, visiting with friends in the daytime and with Butch and Katie in the evenings when they got home from work.

On September 29, we left early, stopping at the first rest area to have breakfast in our Poopsie. We headed for Denver but got stopped for a road check on Vail Pass and had to stop and let Henry cool off again. We arrived at Val and Marlyn's in late afternoon, backed our trailer into their driveway and stayed for a wonderful three-day visit. We looked for a new truck in Denver but didn't find one. We played cards with them and their friends the Davises, and got to see Todd play in a Peewee Baseball League one night. He was so cute; his little legs really made tracks around the baseball diamond.

October 2 we waited for the weather to cool off and took off in the afternoon. We shacked up at Hawk Springs where we spent the night, even though we camped on a side hill. *South Dakota, here we come!* says my diary. We stopped in Edgemont to let Henry cool off and arrived in Rapid City about 4:30. We didn't find the Willeys at home so went to see old friends Bill and Esther Gorendt, parked Poopsie in their driveway and spent the night there. The next morning we went to the sale barn and had breakfast on John Mohn, our niece Paulette's husband. We moved our rig to John and Paulette's driveway and went over to visit Margo, Paulette's mom. She and her friend Bob came over to see our trailer. We all went to Bill and Esther's to greet Francena, a former teacher who had taught all of us either in grade school or high school.

The next morning we ate breakfast at the sale barn again, then hooked on and headed for Sturgis. We didn't have any luck finding a new truck in Rapid City. We parked back of the motel where my brother Frank and Mabel lived; we visited them and with friends around Sturgis.

On October 6 we ate lunch with Frank and Mabel at the truck stop and headed north to my brother Paul and Nordis's place, where we had a delicious chicken dinner and a good visit and watched the Ford-Carter presidential election debate. The next day we were off to Zeona, my birthplace in the sod house. We stopped at my brother Carl and Ruth's ranch first and had a good visit. We stayed all night after we filled our refrigerator with fresh vegetables from Carl's garden.

The next day, we took off for Lemmon to see my sister May and family. We sat and visited till 2:00 a.m. because we had a lot of catching up to do. The next day we gabbed, cleaned house and got ready to go fishing the following day at Shade Hill Reservoir. We had fished there quite a bit when we lived in South Dakota. We loaded up Poopsie and were off to Shade Hill for supper with May and her grandson Jeff.

Sunday, October 10, we fished all day and caught 15 fish; Jeff was the champion fisherman. He caught a big northern pike, I caught a silver bass, and the rest were quite small. My niece Bonnie and husband Virg brought dinner out to the lake. The next day my nephew Dennis and wife Mary Lee stopped in the evening for a visit. The next day we had a long day of restful fishing; Orm caught two trout. That evening, friends Betty and Ray Kolb came with apple pie.

We fished another day and then went to Bison for a delicious supper at Dennis's. The next day we pulled back to Lemmon. We decided to try to get old Henry fixed up so it would run better, and Orm made arrangements to have the valves ground. On October 15 he picked up Henry and drove to Prairie City to see our friend Ralph Hamilton. We had a Pitch game with him and his two daughters.

On October 16, though Henry still gave us some trouble whenever the weather turned warm, we hit the road again, heading for Mobridge, South Dakota, where we parked in John and Donna's back yard for the night. Donna is a sister of our son-on-law, Marlyn. Next day we headed for DeSmet to Marlyn's folks, Clarence and Blanche Stubbe. The weather had cooled off some; it snowed a little and we knew we must get started south soon. It snowed just enough that night in DeSmet that we couldn't get our rig out of the yard till Clarnce hooked on with his tractor and pulled us to the road. But we stopped one more night at Parker at Norm's folks, Rudy and Lucille Johnson. We experienced wonderful hospitality at both places in eastern South Dakota. Rudy took us for a drive out in the country and we found the house where my family and I lived in 1936 and I attended high school as a sophomore. My dad wintered cattle there due to the drought in western South Dakota that year. I enjoyed seeing the town of Parker again and the farm where I once lived years before.

On October 26, we finally started driving south—as far south as we could go into Texas. Our visiting done with family and friends for a while, our adventure began. We chose the closest route from eastern South Dakota straight south on Highway 81. We stayed in Stromsberg, Nebraska, the first night and Salinas, Kansas, the second night.

We stopped at a historic Indian burial ground four miles east of Salinas the next morning. Discovered in 1936, it contains skeletons of 146 Indians that were uncovered and left exactly as placed centuries earlier—in a fixed position, knees drawn up and hands resting close to their faces. Some artifacts were displayed, and we found it to be quite interesting. We stayed in McPherson, Kansas, that night as it was too windy to travel.

The next morning we stopped at Cowtown in Wichita, Kansas, an old tourist attraction. It is an historic group of buildings along the north bank of the Arkansas River. The buildings are over 100 years old; some are restorations while others are replicas. That night we stayed in Blackwell, Oklahoma, in the city park.

October 24, we left Blackwell. We drove through the

beautiful Arbuckle Mountains around Lake Murray near Ardmore, Oklahoma. We drove to Gainesville, Texas, where we camped in a driving rainstorm. We drove through Fort Worth, Texas, and through "Six Flags Over Texas" even though it wasn't open. That night we stayed in Italy, Texas.

The next day we took off for San Antonio and the Alamo. It was destroyed by a hurricane in 1724 and established its present location. The two-story structure was begun in 1727. It became famous as the Long Barrack in the Texas Revolution. The chapel was begun in 1744 and was turned into a fortress in 1835 when the famous battle for the independence of Texas was fought in Mexico. Heroes of the Alamo were William Travis, James Bowie, David Crockett and James Bonham.

We left the Alamo in mid-afternoon and drove to Alice, Texas, where we camped four days in rainy, windy weather. We passed the time by playing cards, looking at old pictures and eating whenever we felt like it. We made a few short trips to Alice for groceries.

On October 30, the sun finally greeted us, so we hooked on and drove to North Padre Island. We walked along the beach, picked up seashells and watched people fishing. Padre Island is 13 miles long, stretching from Corpus Christi almost to Mexico.

Our next destination was Harlingen, the most southern point in Texas. On November 1 we arrived in Harlingen about noon. We went to the chamber of commerce for maps and information about the area, and drove west on Highway 83 where we found lots of RV parks. We stopped and a lady told us she had a vacancy at her place in the country. We followed her to Highland Trailer Court and found our spot to stay for the winter. It was just three miles north of the highway and we parked right under a palm tree in the backyard of the farmhouse, a beautiful spot, quiet and peaceful. Our address was LaFeria, Texas.

On November 12, 1976, Election Day, Jimmy Carter was

elected President of the United States. *We feel better about America now*, I wrote in my diary. We also got our fishing licenses that day to try our luck fishing in Texas. The landlady brought over fresh lemons and avocado salad. What a treat. I made lemon pie the next day and we met some of our neighbors in camp. *This is our first experience at being Snowbirds and so far we love every minute*, my diary says.

We went fishing, enjoyed the sun and made several trips to old Mexico. We ended up staying until May, six months. We spent a lot of time on Padre Island. I gathered so many seashells we barely had room for them in the truck. I worked hard to get the sand cleaned out of them and soaked them in Clorox water, then spread them out in the sun to dry. For pastime, I made some craft items out of them, wall plaques and little animal figures. On Saturday nights we watched the Bob Hope and Carol Burnett shows.

Orm got a job as security guard at the sugar plant just north of our camp and worked enough so we wouldn't have to dip into our savings. We went fishing on South Padre Island where we caught some trout, went out for dinner a few times in the surrounding towns, and played cards or Aggravation in the recreation room with the other Snowbirds. On Thanksgiving, we had a potluck in the recreation room. I made the pumpkin pies and the landlady furnished the turkey.

Christmas was a little lonely for us because it was the first Christmas we had ever spent without at least some of our family. But we made the best of it, did our Christmas shopping and mailed out packages to our kids. We sent out Christmas cards as usual. We spent Christmas Eve listening to some family tapes and music on the radio-tape recorder Ormie bought for us for Christmas. We called the kids and they called us.

~CHAPTER 18~
THE ROAD BACK

We welcomed the new year 1977, talked it over and decided we liked our new nomad lifestyle. I took down the Christmas tree and Orm went to put in his shift at the sugar plant. We had quite a few rainy days through December but passed the time by visiting with our neighbors, going to town and going fishing on sunny days. Even when it rained, the temperature stayed in the 70s and 80s. We enjoyed the fresh pineapple, oranges, and grapefruit we bought at the fruit stands in town.

On January 23 we went with the Carters to Progresso in Mexico, which turned out to be quite an experience. Orm and Frank Carter each bought a bottle of booze. When we started back across the border, a Mexican customs officer tapped Orm on the shoulder.

"You have to come into the office and sign a card," he said.

"What's going on?" I asked, following them.

"You are only allowed one quart per person per month," the officer explained, "and you look mighty familiar. Sign this card."

"Well, I might look familiar to you, but I haven't bought any booze across the border since the first time I was here, and that was way back in November. I'm not signing anything,"

The officer finally believed him and let him go. Whew!

That was our last trip into Mexico there. In February, we finally got sick of the rain and made plans for Orm to work till the 15th of March and we would leave on the 25th. Anxious to continue our adventure, we worked hard getting our RV all cleaned up inside and outside. Orm got our radiator fixed, and finished up at his job. After we went to Harlingen to turn in his "monkey suit" (uniform), we spent two interesting hours at the Confederate Air Force Museum, which had airplanes and memorabilia from World War II. Monday, May 21, was moving day. We headed for North Padre Island and Corpus Christi, camped right on the beach and went for a long walk. The weather was beautiful, warm enough for shorts. It made us happy to be on the road again.

The next morning we pulled out at 9:00 and got about five miles out when we heard a noise in Henry's engine. Orm stopped and put the hood up. Several people stopped to offer help, but finally he got it going and at 1:00 we limped into the Ford garage at Corpus Christi, prepared to sit right there in the garage lot till they got Henry fixed, overnight if necessary. But at 3:00 p.m. we were on our way and it only cost us $24 for a broken lifter. Luck was in our corner again. We went back to Padre Island and Port Aransas where we had plans to meet the Carters. We parked right across the street from them.

We caught up with the Suttzers and Johnsons, too, people we had met in LaFeria, at Port Lavaca State Park. Francis and Dorothy Suttzer decided to travel with us for a while. Si and Leona Johnson left for Wisconsin, and the rest of us did some beachcombing for a couple days before we left the area. We traveled as far as Rollover Pass on the gulf, where we fished out of the back of the trailer. I caught a sheephead fish and Orm skinned his leg getting it netted for me. The next night we each caught a nice flounder and I lost a big red fish when he snapped my line. We had one flounder for supper; it just fit in my big cast iron skillet and it tasted great.

Easter Sunday, April 10, the four of us went out to dinner

on the pier to Gulf Haven, where we all had the seafood platter with a little of everything, all fresh and very delicious.

On the 13th, we reluctantly left Rollover Pass, Louisiana-bound. We drove through Port Arthur's mammoth oil refineries and crossed the big causeway and bridge into Louisiana. The Suttzers traveled with us to Louisiana and then left us to go home to Michigan. That night we stayed in a rest area, and the next morning went into Port Charles to get a part for Henry. That night we stayed on Lake Ponchartrain.

The next night we camped in Biloxi, Mississippi, parked by the tourist information booth. We watched people on the beach sunbathing and swimming and saw a lot of shrimp and fishing boats. We did some beachcombing but found no shells.

On April 18 we left Pass Christian, Mississippi, headed for Alabama. We stopped for the night in the town park in Grove Hill, Alabama, a nice spot with beautiful weather and wonderful scenic country. We went to bed to find out the next morning the police had locked us in the park for the night. We wondered if we would be able to travel, but by the time we ate our breakfast someone came to unlock the gate.

We took off and drove to Mound State Park at Moundsville and checked in with one other camper there. We toured the Indian mounds museum and gift shop, cleaned our trailer and Henry, and Orm built a little porch for outside our door, only to pull out and leave it the next day. We decided that CRS (Can't Remember Sh--) Disease was already setting in and we hadn't hit 60 yet.

On April 20 we pulled into Decatur, Alabama, where we visited two of my nieces, Deloris and Frances, and their families. We backed our trailer into Deloris and Tommy's driveway and had a great visit there. They took us on a tour of their city, and one night we went over to Frances and Ron's house for supper around their swimming pool. The hospitality was wonderful, but on the 25th we headed out again, Kentucky-bound. We pulled into Tennessee and decided to stay over and check out my old stomping grounds at Ft. Oglethorpe, Georgia. We drove around the loop on Lookout Mountain, which hasn't changed since I was there in 1944. The next day we drove to Ft. Oglethorpe and Chickamauga Chattanooga Military Park, where I had spent 20 months during World War II. Oglethorpe was now just a small town, and there was not much left of the old fort. I couldn't even place the barracks I'd lived in when I was stationed there.

On April 27 we entered Kentucky about noon. We arrived in Raceland to my sister Ruth and Tob's place, where we caught up on visiting, went fishing and enjoyed my sister's good cooking. While there, we drove to Fredericksburg, Virginia, to visit my brother Bill and Frances. We also made a side trip with Ruth and Tob to Thelma, Kentucky, to visit their daughter Adele and family.

On May 12 we took off for Dakota and points west. Butch and Katie had their wedding planned for June 3 in Rock Springs, Wyoming, and we wanted to be there. Over the next several days, we made our way across the Midwest, through Ohio, Indiana, Illinois and Iowa. Somewhere out of Galeseburg, Illinois, Henry stopped dead in his tracks. Orm worked for an hour and a half but it wouldn't start, so he walked a quarter mile up the road and brought back a mechanic with a new coil, and in 15 minutes it was running again. But we only went one mile and it quit again.

"Need some help?" a guy hollered as he stopped beside us. He was a nice black fellow named Glenn and we caught a ride with him into Woodhull, seven miles away. Orm bought a new condenser and a used coil. Glenn insisted on taking us back to our rig. Orm tried to pay him, but finally had to put a ten-dollar bill in his pocket. We headed down the road again, stopped at Hoover's birthplace at West Branch and stayed at a camp at Cedar Falls, Iowa.

The next morning we stopped at the Little Brown Church

in the Vale, still in Iowa, built in 1804. We arrived in Northfield, Minnesota, and surprised our old friends, Ida and Cliff Greenfield, former neighbors in Boulder Canyon. We played golf, cards and Scrabble and had a good visit with Cliff and Ida and their family.

We left Norhfield on May 17, bound for Lemmon, South Dakota, to visit my sister May. We stayed there until the last of May, had a good visit with barbecues and saw all her family. From there we traveled to Bison and Prairie City to visit Grandma and Ralph Hamilton. We met the whole Willey family in Rapid City, where we parked again at Paulette and Johns. We had a nice little family reunion there. Everyone in the original family still living came: Grandma, Noble and Marge, Gladys and Jack, Bonnie and Russ, Margo and Orm and I. While parked there we made trips to Spearfish and Sturgis to visit relatives, and to Deadwood to sell our remaining lots in Boulder Canyon.

~Chapter 19~
Our Son's Wedding
and We Land in Oregon

We took off on May 31, bound for Rock Springs, Wyoming, for Butch and Katie's wedding on June 3. We put four new tires on Poopsie in Gillette, Wyoming, and Henry seemed to be running well. In hot and windy Rock Springs the relatives arrived for the wedding: Bonnie and Russ, Grandma Willey, Val and Marlyn and kids from Denver, and Marlene, Norm and boys from California. Butch and Katie had a beautiful ceremony and then a reception at the community recreation hall. We saw the honeymooners off for Jackson, Wyoming. Val, Marlene and I moved all the food and drinks to their house, and the next morning our family cleaned up the recreation hall before the girls and their families left for home.

When Butch and Katie came back from their honeymoon, the four of us went to Flaming Gorge for a little fishing vacation. We fished together one day, caught some nice trout and had a big fish fry together in our trailer. They stayed all night and went home the next morning. It turned windy out at the lake, and after another night we decided to go back to Rock Springs, where Katie fixed a nice turkey dinner and the next night Butch took us out to dinner.

On Sunday, June 12, our 34th anniversary, we hit the road again, this time headed for Denver and Val and Marlyn's. We parked our trailer in their driveway until the 23rd, watched Todd play peewee baseball, made new curtains for the trailer, went to two big flea markets and made plans to meet Carl, Ruth and May at Ft. Peck Dam in Montana. Grandpa and Todd went fishing one day while Val and I went shopping.

We had made plans to meet Carl, Ruth, Ben, May and Jeff at Ft. Peck Dam, so on June 23, we hit the road again. We left in a hailstorm and traveled slowly because of the heat and the hail. The next day we arrived at Custer Battlefield but didn't stay long because of the heat. On June 28 we went to the VA in Miles City, Montana, to get antibiotics for my tongue infection. We finally got to Ft. Peck, set up camp and waited for the South Dakota bunch to arrive. When they got there the next day, the long-awaited visit began. We did a lot of fishing every day and had some good picnics together. May and Jeff decided to go home on the 4th of July, and Carl and Ruth stayed to travel with us for a while.

Diary entry: *July 6, our first anniversary on the road, a lot cooler than it was a year ago when we took off for California. We made a few tracks across the United States, east and west and north and south. We had some great experiences – some good and some bad, but mostly good. We don't plan to settle down yet, a lot of country we haven't seen, but have hit 26 states in a year.*

Traveling westward again, we stopped at the pioneer museum in Glasgow, Montana, stayed at the Nelson Reservoir under the trees out of the wind, and decided to stay the night. The next day we explored the old mining town of Zortman and took a side trip to Landusky and south to the Missouri River to the wildlife refuge road. We camped right on the river and fished in the evening. We spent one more day there, and then drove to Lewistown. We got in the car with Ben, Carl and Ruth and drove to see the ghost towns of Gilt Edge and Maiden.

July 12 we broke camp again and headed for Great Falls, Montana. We stopped to see the Sodbusters Museum between

Mocassin and Windham; it was a good one. From there we went to Ft. Benton to look over that area.

On July 15, Carl, Ruth and Ben decided they had to go home, so reluctantly we parted company. We headed west and they headed home to Zeona, South Dakota. We continued west through East Glacier Park and Libby, Montana, where Orm fished on the Yaak River near Libby. Grand Coulee was our next stop, where we took pictures and relaxed awhile. We stayed all night at Wenatchee, Washington, after Orm stopped along the road looking for rocks and found and killed a rattlesnake among the rocks. The next night we drove into Spokane, Washington, where we spent the night in a rest area.

We stopped in Startup, Washington, where we stayed for a couple days, cleaned up our trailer and truck and rested up. We visited old friends, Ray Merkle and his wife, in Marysville for an overnight. He and Orm had served together in the Black Hills at a CCC camp years before. The next day we took off to Fort Canby State Park on the Oregon coast. On July 27 we pulled into Carol and Chuck's yard in Tualatin, Oregon—not planning to stay, but stay we did, and have been in Oregon ever since, except for another two years on the road from September 1988 to October 1990.

We went back and forth to Hillsboro, Oregon, to visit Grandma and Bon and Russ. Ruth and Tob came while we visited there. We had a big family picnic at Carol and Chuck's for Ruth and Tob. We had some wonderful times while we were parked there in Carol and Chuck's yard, but we decided to settle down in Oregon for a while.

On September 18 we moved to North Plains, Oregon, where we took care of the Holiday RV Center for my nephew Boyd. We bought a little furniture and some appliances and moved into the two-bedroom apartment there on the premises.

In our year on the road we didn't see all 50 states, but 28 of them and a little of old Mexico. Twenty-two thousand miles later and Henry was still running (barely, sometimes), but

Poopsie needed some repairs. The roof leaked, the 12-volt system quit and even the little TV quit us. We sold them both, and the last time we saw Henry it was stalled on the road between North Plains and Hillsboro. It had quit us so many times it was good to know that someone else would have to try to figure him out.

~CHAPTER 20~
WE SETTLE IN OREGON

When we landed in Oregon in July of 1977 we had no intentions of staying. But the month of August went by while my sweetie was getting his health problems checked out at the Veterans Administration Hospital. He had dizzy spells at night and also equilibrium problems. Doctors examined him and gave him persantine and aspirin. In the interim, my nephew Boyd wanted someone to live on his place at North Plains and manage his RV storage center. He offered us a deal we couldn't refuse.

On September 18 we pulled Poopsie out to the new place, moved out of Poopsie into the apartment and got settled in our new place with the new job. It was an easy job, but we found it very confining until Boyd got someone to rent the upstairs apartment. The renters relieved us when we wanted to get away for a few hours.

While we lived at Holiday RV Center, we made a trip to California with the little pickup camper we bought after we sold Poopsie. Carol and Chuck went with us as far as Reno, where we parted company; they went over one mountain to San Francisco and we went over the Sierras to visit our relatives in Lancaster, California. It was a tough trip; we followed the snowplow out of Carson City to LeeVining, where we were stalled overnight because snow closed the road. The next morning we followed the snowplow out, finally reaching Lancaster in late afternoon.

About the same time we decided to stay in Oregon,

Marlene and Norm moved to Corvallis, Oregon. They lived in a motel while their home was built in northwest Corvallis, where they still live today.

The first night we stayed at the Holiday RV Center I was awakened by something running over my stomach. I just knew it was that big rat we had heard in the walls earlier. Sure enough, after I got up I discovered he had eaten part of the azalea Marlene had brought me. The next morning we went to town and armed ourselves with rat traps and poison and placed them under the dishwasher where we had heard the noises. Then we closed off all the holes we could find and baited the traps every night. But he ate the bait off night after night and avoided getting caught.

Thanksgiving rolled around and we invited the Willey family — Grandma, Bonnie and Russ, Gladys and Jack, Noble and Marge, and Marlene and Norm — for dinner. While we ate dinner, we heard the trap snap under the cupboard. Finally we outsmarted that rat and it was the end of the rat episode.

Butch and Katie flew out from Rock Springs to spend Christmas with us that year. We had a great time, invited all the Ruby relatives in for a poker party and enjoyed opening Christmas presents with Butch and Katie on Christmas Eve.

The next summer Val , Marlyn, their kids and his folks, Clarence and Blanche, came in one car for a visit. We rented one of the motor homes at the RV center and took them to the beach one day and enjoyed their visit.

We stayed at the Holiday RV Center exactly one year, and Boyd promised to give us a commission if we could sell it for him. Orm found a buyer, so we had to think about moving again. Our travel trailer was gone, as was old Henry. We bought a small motor home, but we didn't think it had enough room to go on the road again. Besides, we kind of liked it here in this beautiful state and decided to buy a mobile home somewhere and settle down. We found our little mobile home in Thunderbird Park at Wilsonville, south of Portland. We had another yard sale to get rid of some of the stuff we didn't need, including the chord organ I had bought from Margie. I enjoyed playing it a lot, but I sold it to a sweet old lady who wanted it to limber up her arthritic fingers.

We found our new home, a comfortable little place in a nice park with a recreation hall and swimming pool. Chuck and Carol hired us to work at their sign business, Signs in Depth, and we both worked there for almost a year. I cut Styrofoam letters with a hot wire machine and sanded and painted them, and Orm went out to sell signs. We enjoyed the work and they paid us well.

Our grandson Jesse was born October 18, 1978, and in early spring we decided to take Amtrak to Rock Springs to meet him for the first time. Butch talked about quitting his work in the coal mine and moving to Oregon. Of course that pleased us, and when they sold their house that fall, they came.

We liked the sign business so much we decided to start one of our own. We couldn't go into competition with Carol and Chuck, so decided to move farther south to Eugene, Oregon. We sold our mobile home at a little loss after a year, but found our new one at Fern Ridge Mobile Estates west of Eugene. It was a little bigger and we had beautiful flowers and a nice garden spot on the edge of a large filbert orchard.

Butch and Katie arrived from Wyoming and we decided to open our sign shop together. They rented a house with a garage and we opened our business in their garage. It took awhile but we soon got enough jobs that the garage didn't have enough room to make large signs. We rented a place in an industrial complex and set up our shop in earnest in 1980. The kids brought Jesse to work with them every day. We got him a little desk and he played for hours at his desk. We enjoyed him a lot. Time passed and it was soon obvious the business wasn't enough to support all of us, so Butch and Katie got jobs elsewhere. Butch continued to help Orm install signs when we needed him. We kept the business going on a cash basis and just started getting repeat business when I began to have some health problems.

~Chapter 21~
Our Angel Arrives

On August 1, 1980, an angel came to our family. Her name is Kristamae. She is our granddaughter, the daughter of Butch and Katie. At first I wondered why our family was blessed with a severely handicapped child, but we no longer question it because we love her so much just the way she is. Our Kristamae is a source of joy to her grandfather and me in spite of the fact she doesn't talk to us and can never run, play with dolls or do all the other things little girls do. She shows us her love with her eyes and her beautiful smile, and that is enough for us. We love her very much, and we are absolutely *certain* she loves us too. Kristamae is our angel girl.

The first year of Krista's life was normal and uneventful. But when she didn't walk by the time she was 15 months old, her parents feared something was wrong. They began multiple visits to doctors and to the University of Oregon Hospital in search of answers. At first she was diagnosed as mildly retarded, but she later developed other symptoms. She became floppy and unbalanced. She began vomiting and passing out. Before long she lost interest in toys, and the doll we had given her for her first birthday was left untouched. She cried most nights, obviously in pain at times. Doctors tried many different drugs for her seizures and other problems, but still no answers. What was wrong with our little angel girl?

The next diagnosis came across as epileptic with cerebral palsy. She had to have braces for her legs to help her instability. When Kristamae reached her fourth birthday, we still didn't have any answers. Finally they took her to the crippled children division of the hospital, and her final diagnosis was Rett Syndrome. It's a degenerative disease that occurs only in little girls. The neurological disorder strikes randomly 1 in 10,000 girls within the first two years of life. Some of the symptoms are loss of verbal language, stereotypical hand movements, a wide-based and stiff-legged walk, shakiness of torso and limbs, scoliosis, seizures, abnormal sleep patterns, constipation, and teeth grinding.

There is no cure for Rett Syndrome, the doctors said. The outcome of this disease is a lifetime of full-time care, even for the most basic needs. Patients face a lifetime of dependency issues and general care.

Butch and Katie, Kristamae's parents, educated themselves and saw that she got every kind of therapy available. Dedicated parents, they were dogged in their determination to give their daughter the same benefits available to other kids. They took her to regular classes with other kids and took part in all the activities she was capable of doing.

Today Kristamae is 25 years old, and although they told us she wouldn't live to be a teenager, she now lives in a group home where she gets 24-hour care. It was a tough decision to move her out of their home, but Butch and Katie found it difficult to give her the care she needs and still carry on their normal activities and jobs. She will always be our angel, and when we go to see her, she blesses us with her wonderful smiles.

Still working in our sign business in 1981, we experienced an illness we hadn't counted on. I was 61 and in the prime of my life. Orman and I worked designing, making and installing signs around town. We both loved the work. We cut letters out of Styrofoam, sanded and painted them, and installed them. The business did quite well, and I loved the work so much I could hardly wait to get to work every morning.

But one morning about 6:00 I awoke with pains in my chest. The pain came and went with a rhythm much the same way I remembered labor pains at a much younger age. I tried to ignore them, but they returned much too often. On the way to work that morning we stopped at a clinic for a checkup, even though the pains finally subsided. An electrocardiogram revealed nothing, but after some blood work and giving the doctor my family history, he made the diagnosis.

"You must stop smoking if you wish to continue living. You are having some heart trouble," the doctor said. He gave me a little bottle of nitroglycerin tablets to put under my tongue for chest pain. The diagnosis stunned me, and at first I experienced denial. I really didn't believe the doctor knew for sure. When I got in the car, I promptly lit up a cigarette (to calm my nerves, I told myself).

Two months passed, and two or three times I took the nitro pills when I felt heaviness in my chest. I never had the pain again, just shortness of breath and a heavy feeling that felt like an elephant leaned on me.

Willing to do anything to feel better, after about ten days I promised myself to give up cigarettes for good. I contacted the American Lung Association, which sent me a pamphlet that explained how to stop smoking in 20 days. I was determined to quit this time and followed their guidelines. I used a journal to write down my thoughts whenever I had the urge to smoke, and I smoked my last cigarette 18 days later. It was one of the toughest things I ever did in my life, but it gave me hope for a new chance for life. Also, I began to feel better.

Three months after my visit to the doctor, I went to work one morning, busily gluing letters onto a sign I had painted the day before. I sat down at the table to work, when suddenly I felt a heavy, burning sensation in my chest. When it radiated to my arms and hands and finally up into my neck and jaws, I collapsed in a lawn chair and Orman called 911. I went to the hospital by ambulance.

Ormie called Butch and he came to the hospital. They loaded me in his car and took me to the Roseburg VA Hospital, where I spent two weeks recuperating. After some damage to my heart, I learned to live a less stressful life along with a sensible diet and a routine schedule of exercise and walking. I enjoyed doing any activity I liked at a more relaxed pace.

In all the years since, I haven't lit up one cigarette. I have been tempted a few times, but I have a wonderful smoke-free life and am no longer a victim of a dirty, senseless habit.

~Chapter 22~
Slab City, a Free Place in the Sun

After my heart attack, we sold our Signs 'n' Stuff business. Orman stayed home with me for a while, but finally decided to get a job. He left one Friday morning and came home in the afternoon.

"I go to work Monday morning," he announced. He landed a job in Junction City as maintenance man at the nursing home there. He liked the job, and before long we decided to move to Junction City to save the drive every day. We hated to leave our beautiful spot in the filbert orchard, but we thought it the sensible thing to do at the time.

So in 1985 w got settled and felt contented in our little apartment in Junction City, where Orman could walk to work. I got acquainted with other residents in the complex and spent a lot of time playing cards and meeting my friends to crochet. We sold our camp trailer and bought a used Avion trailer, and then we planned a trip to southern California and Arizona.

The trip to the deserts of the Southwest in the winter of 1986 was a once-in-a-lifetime vacation. There aren't enough adjectives to describe the low desert in southern California and Arizona. It is Indian summer there all winter, with hard-to-describe sunsets and a calm desert climate. Daytime temperatures ranged in the high 70s or low 80s.

The day we arrived on the desert in mid-January, we looked forward to the spring-like atmosphere. After a 1200-mile trip from our home in Oregon to the Slabs of California, we prepared to relax. We drove through Oregon's rain and northern California's fog, and didn't see the sun until we broke over the Tehachapi Pass north of Mojave. When we reached Slab City we unloaded our lawn recliners and stretched out in the sun. And to think we had two months of this ahead of us.

Three miles east of Niland is a place called Slab City, so named because of the cement slabs left there when a military base was abandoned in the early 50s. We were told more than 4,000 motor homes and travel trailers parked there the year before, and this year they moved in and out daily. It was a dirty place to camp—no grass, just sagebrush and sand around the slabs. However, we had no camping fees to pay, and the weather alone made it worth staking our claim for a while. The nights were chilly but not cold enough to require the use of our furnace in the month we camped there.

Slab City is a warm place in the sun where many retired folks go to give up all the conveniences of home, a place where there's no electricity, no water, no paved roads and no stores. We sacrifice all these conveniences to enjoy the sunny climate all winter. The most noise we heard there was the hum of the trailer generators running to charge up the batteries, making it possible to enjoy some semblance of the home conveniences we left behind.

Some called this place "Senile City" because most of the people there were retired and in their late 60s, 70s and 80s. When I heard some of the chatter on our CB, I thought some of them had been there in the sun too long. Reminds me of a sign I saw on the back of a motor home: WE ARE NOT SENIOR CITIZENS, WE ARE JUST RECYCLED TEENAGERS. Another read: I HAVE WAITED ALL THESE YEARS TO GET OLD SO I COULD REMINISCE ABOUT THE OLD DAYS,

AND NOW THAT I'M OLD, I CAN'T REMEMBER A DARN THING! Or this one: WE ARE SPENDING OUR KIDS' INHERITANCE.

A lot of full-time RVers lived at the Slabs, including about 300 LOWS (Loners on Wheels). Every weekend we attended a large flea market on Main Street with about 200 vendors. We enjoyed the fresh fruits and vegetables we got there — tomatoes, cucumbers, cauliflower, broccoli, radishes, green onions, asparagus, grapefruit, tangerines, oranges, huge avocados and cantaloupe — all at reasonable prices. Everything was fresh out of the field or orchard. I ate so many grapefruits I'm surprised I didn't turn into one. I defy anyone to peel one of those fresh tangerines without squirting some of that juice in your eye.

The days passed quickly with either fishing or staying around camp to do chores. We stayed busy most of the time, visiting with our RV neighbors outdoors and relaxing in our lawn chairs. The sun gave us the most spectacular show as it sank behind the Chocolate Mountains in the west. Some nights we had potluck together and sat around the campfire telling each other tales. Or we had a game of cards in one of the trailers. We roasted marshmallows on our campfire and stuffed ourselves with camp pies. We had found the special irons at a flea market; we put two slices of bread with any kind of fruit or pie mix between the slices, buttered them on the outside, closed the two-sided iron and stuck it in the campfire. We turned them often with the long handle and when they were a luscious brown, they melted in our mouths. After we ate, one lady brought out her guitar, a man emerged from his trailer with his fiddle and we all sang. When our voices gave out we talked until the fire died down and the desert air was too cool to sit outdoors. It's hard to beat the feeling of fellowship when gathering around a campfire in the evening with the full moon lighting the surroundings.

We went to town only for groceries and water and to do our laundry. We parked close to the Coachella Canal and spent a lot of time fishing for catfish. We caught a few, but fishing didn't live up to our expectations. Our new friends from California showed us a new place to fish in the Salton Sea. We spent the day with them and hit the jackpot. We carried about 30 pounds of fish back to camp—four sargo, one tilapia and three large corvena. We ate the tilapia for supper that night, and if there's a better fish anywhere, I'd have to be shown.

Campers at Slab City followed the custom of digging a hole in the sand to make their own septic system. We hesitated to do this because of unsanitary conditions, but discovered that if they are covered properly there is no odor and the sand makes a natural septic system. It saved running to town to dump when the holding tank filled up.

What a life we had. Upon arising in the morning, we took our coffee outside to sit in the sun and opened the door to let the sun warm up the trailer. Before long I pulled the shades on the south and west to keep it cool. We walked down the canal, watched the huge carp lazily making their way downstream and wondered why the catfish didn't show themselves. Was it because they were scarce or because they were smart enough to know we were waiting for them?

The men in camp went to the desert each morning to get a pickup load of wood to burn in the rock fireplace they built in the center of our group of Oregon RVs. We ladies stayed in camp to catch up on cleaning chores, cooking, correspondence, crafts or whatever else we felt like doing.

I was so fascinated by Slab City and the surrounding area I picked up information at the Chamber of Commerce. Slab City is near the Salton Sea, which stretches 35 miles long from Mecca almost to Calipatria; it is 12 miles wide and 50 feet deep. The water surface is 235 feet below sea level. In the 15th century Salton Sea was a freshwater body called Lake Cahuilla by the Indians who lived on its shores. Fed by the Colorado River, it stretched from Mexicalli on the south to Indio on the north; on the west from Superstition Mountains to a point east of Niland. At that time the water's surface was 40 feet above sea level.

At the beginning of the 16th century, the Colorado River changed course. Lake Cahuilla began to dry up. By 1774 the lake was completely dry. The sea began to fill in rapidly in the late 1800s. It quickly covered railroad tracks that had been built. To this day they lie at the bottom of the Salton Sea.

The Salton Sea as it is today was formed when the Colorado River broke its banks south of Yuma in 1905. From 1905 to 1907 the river caused unusually high floods. The sea is presently fed by the Alamo and New Rivers, as well as irrigation drainage water from the All American Canal. During the 1920s its elevation was around 250 feet below sea level.

The little town of Niland has an interesting history. In 1877, the Southern Pacific Railroad built its line from Los Angeles to Yuma. The Niland station was just a whistle stop, then called Old Beach. In 1906 the name was changed to Imperial Junction. It was there that the pioneers from the east and other parts of the country arrived by train and had their first glimpse of the desert they would later call home.

In March of 1914 Niland was ushered into being with a blare of trumpets. Imperial Junction became Niland, with reference to the valley of the Nile River and the fertility of the land surrounding the city.

The town of Calipatria, 12 miles south of Niland, is the "lowest down city" in the western hemisphere. It is 185 feet below sea level. The American flag in town flies at sea level, at the top of a 180-foot flagpole.

Since we visited the Slabs on 1996, we have been informed that Slab City no longer exists as such. It has been purchased by a developer who plans to build a large modern RV park, so I'm sure hundreds of RVers will miss their free place in the sun.

~CHAPTER 23~
COLORADO RIVER PARADISE

From Slab City we moved across the desert to the Colorado River east of Brawley. The gorgeous desert with its seven-mile stretch of sand dunes lies in the center of the Chocolate Mountains. It's easy to see how they got their name with their different shades of chocolate as the sun shines on the varied formations. We stayed at the Palo Verde County Park right on the river, backing our trailer almost to the water. Before supper we already had our fishing lines in place, sitting on our lawn chairs watching the brilliant sunset. The fish weren't biting, but it was a wonderful place to relax. The next day was windy and cool, but we stayed another night just to enjoy that beautiful place. We vowed to return again someday.

We took off to Arizona and east from Blythe to Quartsite, where the giant saguaro cactus reach their arms to the sky, and where the rock hounds dot the landscape with their motor homes and trailers. The desert shrubbery and cactus are unique; they are found only in this part of our country. Besides the saguaro and the Joshua trees, the ocotillo cactus caught my eye. Sometimes called coachwhip, Jacob's staff or vine cactus, it grows to a height of 20 feet, has a prickly wand-like stem and bears clusters of scarlet flowers at the tips of its stems.

At Quartsite we found the annual giant swap meet; if you stayed two weeks you would never find time to see it all. We found acres and acres of everything from gems to junk lining the streets.

Next it was back to California and the Colorado River, stalking the catfish as we traveled north from Blythe. It's a paradise for "snowbirds," with resort after resort from the wide place in the road called Earp as far north as Lake Havisu City. Most of the RV camps are located on the river and we lucked out a couple times to park our rig a stone's throw from the river. This was the kind of camping we liked. If we got hungry while fishing we could step into the trailer for a snack, or if we felt the urge for a nap, we could sack out close to our fishing lines.

We followed the Colorado River on the California side as far as Parker Dam, where we crossed over to Arizona. We had many views of spectacular scenery, the river with a backdrop of the Whipple Mountains. We explored some of the Arizona state parks on the way to Lake Havisu City, where we found the famous London Bridge, a unique tourist trap.

How did London Bridge get to Arizona from England? It was one of several bridges that spanned the Thames River. It was dismantled because it started falling down and was shipped across the Atlantic to its new site spanning the Colorado River at a cost of more than seven million dollars. Underneath the bridge are shops of all kinds and amusements for tourists: a two-hour river queen ride, paddleboats, a theater, restaurants, a candle factory, a candy shop where we watched them make taffy, and many others. We walked up a long flight of stairs to the top of the bridge, walked the length of the bridge on top and down the steps on the other side to the shops and parking area. You can also drive across London Bridge.

Our journey took us westward again, across the high desert, where we stayed by the side of the road at Vidal Junction, California, and the next night at a supermarket parking lot at Lucerne Valley. We stocked up on groceries and did our laundry there. We headed for Silverwood State Park in the San Bernadino Mountains. Due to the rainy, windy weather, the park was closed at the lower level near the lake where the altitude was over 4,000 feet. We decided to seek warmer territory, with plans to return sometime in the summer.

Orm pulled our big rig over crooked, foggy mountain roads, and when we hit the freeway, we headed for the desert only to drive through one of the worst sand blizzards I had ever seen. We arrived at Saddle Back Butte State Park east of Lancaster, California. It was a primitive park with no hookups, but they did have water and a dumping station and we had our generator to furnish us with electricity. We decided to stay until the wind subsided.

The next morning the sun came out and we headed north toward home in Oregon. After staying one night in Fresno, we ran into heavy rains and wind. We stopped at a campground south of Sacramento just minutes before Interstate 5 closed ahead of us due to flooding. Held up for two days, we listened constantly to the latest reports on the radio about flooded areas, closed highways, 24,000 people evacuating their homes and warnings about the worst storm northern California had experienced in 30 years.

Finally we decided to head out, finding our way around the floodwaters, going back south to Stockton, then west on 580 to 680 and north to Highway 12. Crossing the Sacramento River at Walnut Creek, we drove through foot-deep water. We decided to travel Highway 101 north from Santa Rosa, only to find out it was closed farther north due to mudslides. We detoured back to Interstate 5, zigzagging our way across California to get home.

The deserts in Arizona and southern California and the Colorado River made our winter vacation enjoyable in spite of the road and weather conditions to get there and home again. We vowed to do our traveling earlier in the fall and stay longer in the spring.

After a year at Northtown in our small apartment, we

wanted a little more room and moved again, this time to a two-bedroom place on Main Street where it was a close walk to town. We lived in Junction City almost three years and met our new friends, Will and Lois Glenn, and Roy and Lois Zilko.

That year, 1987, we decided to go to Ohio for Christmas via Amtrak. We made reservations for a round trip with three major stops, one to visit sister-in-law Frances in Fredericksburg, Virginia, another to visit my sister Ruth in Nicholasville, Kentucky, and the last stop at Val and Terry's in Belpre, Ohio.

~CHAPTER 24~
COAST TO COAST ON AMTRAK

We waited for the train impatiently, as it was an hour late. Finally we heard the whistle blow as the train rumbled to a grinding halt in Eugene, Oregon.

"All aboard!" the conductor shouted. Our enthusiasm returned and we hurried onto the super liner, the *Coast Starlight*, and settled in to enjoy our long trip to the east coast. Since Christmas was just weeks away, we anticipated the Christmas decorations in every little town on Amtrak's route across America.

The train rolled along, showing us the familiar sights of Oregon while we had lunch in the dining car. We changed trains in Portland and boarded another super liner, which we rode all the way to Chicago. After the evening meal, we settled down for our first night in our reclining chairs. We got some sleep, but we got interrupted by children running up and down the aisle, the occasional whimper of a baby, and some inconsiderate people who enjoyed visiting with each other all night long. In Spokane, Washington, we had a 45-minute layover while they hooked our car to the eastbound *Empire Builder* from Seattle.

"Breakfast is being served in the diner," the porter announced as he walked through our car. We survived our first night. We roused up out of our nests to freshen up in the restrooms before breakfast. As we ate, it slowly turned daylight and we floated through a vast area of Christmas trees beautifully decorated with shiny blankets of snow and ice. As we crossed the Flathead River along the southern edge of Glacier National Park, we saw some spectacular sights. Three elk pricked up their ears as we invaded their primitive territory. We crossed the Rocky Mountains, majestic as they towered above the snow-filled valley, and watched the river curving its way to lower elevations. We got to the summit called Mariah Pass, a little more then 5,000 feet high, the lowest railroad pass over the Rocky Mountains. Then we rolled down the other side and across endless miles of plains in Montana, North Dakota, and into Minnesota. The sun shone brightly on the snow-covered prairie on a beautiful winter day.

Quite a few passengers left us at different stations, which gave us empty seats to stretch out in. We woke up pulling into St. Paul, Minnesota. It was another nice, sunny morning, but passengers boarding told us the chill factor was 20 degrees below zero. We didn't care because we were happily snuggled in our seats on Amtrak.

A few hours later, as we pulled into Union Station in Chicago, the tapering Hancock Building came into view and the Sears Tower, once the tallest building in the world, dominated the skyline. Many other skyscrapers appeared as we approached the station. We had four hours to kill before catching our next train. The old depot looked much the same as it did 47 years before when we traveled through while on furlough during the war, either on our way home or going back to military camp. We ate and browsed through a few shops. It was nice to have our land legs back for a while and we did a lot of walking.

We boarded the *Capitol Limited*, which took us to Washington, D.C. We rode in the dome car quite awhile between Chicago and Washington. As it got daylight, it was a gray day. The train wound along the river, and sometimes when we rounded a curve we could see most of the cars ahead of us, resembling a long snake curling itself around the hills and along the stream. We pulled into Cumberland, Maryland, about noon with the snow blowing hard. A few passengers got out to play in the snow for a few minutes. We arrived in Washington about 45 minutes late and had to hurry to catch our train to Fredericksburg, Virginia. We managed to see the Lincoln Memorial, the Washington Monument and the Smithsonian Building from the train.

We had traveled through 14 states. What a privilege to sit there gazing out the window at a continuous panoramic view of our beautiful America, from the winter green of Oregon to our nation's capital. As anticipated, we saw many small towns as the train made its whistle stops to take on passengers or let some off. The Christmas spirit was evident across America in the lighting displays we witnessed.

We boarded the *Silver Star* for the last leg of our trip, the first stop on our tour being Fredericksburg, Virginia. We visited there with sister-in-law Frances and had the opportunity to tour the historic area, including a visit to the Quantico National Cemetery where my brother Bill was buried. Ann, Jerry, Jean and Sam, Frances's grown children, came one evening to cook dinner for us and we enjoyed a poker game with them for old time's sake.

Three days later, we jumped on the rail again, this time on the *Potomac* to catch the *Cardinal* in Washington to travel all the way back to Chicago with two stops in between. In the diner between Stanton and Clifton Gorge, Virginia, we had a dinner of vegetable lasagna, salad, buns and coffee.

Our second stop was Prince, West Virginia, where we arrived on schedule. We had five days to visit my sister Ruth. She lived next door to her daughter Adele, her husband Jim and their three children. Adele invited us over to their house for dinner every night.

We went back to Prince to catch our train to Charleston, our third scheduled stop, to spend nine days, which included

Christmas, with our daughter and family. Val had met and married Terry McGee, but they held up their reception until we arrived. We enjoyed meeting all of Terry's folks, and a few days later we spent Christmas with them again in Pennsboro, West Virginia.

After the holiday, we began our return trip to Oregon. We boarded the *Cardinal* again in Charleston, where some of the personnel on the train recognized and greeted us. We had breakfast east of Indianapolis the next morning, and about 10:00 a.m. the train stopped dead in her tracks. About 10 hours out of Chicago we had lost our power; the heat went off and it started snowing. We put on our coats and covered up with our blankets as did everyone else. Soon repairmen came in a van and the train moved again. We limped into Chicago two hours late, had a sandwich in Union Station and got on the *Empire Builder* once more headed for Seattle and home.

Between Tomah and LaCrosse, Wisconsin, we went through the little town of Sparta, which is a special place to us because it was the mustering-out place for my husband after World War II. He had his discharge in hand when we left there in 1945. Sparta is also the place we met for the first time after the war. When we left LaCrosse, we crossed the Mississippi River into Minnesota. For 140 miles we saw fertile farmlands and small riverbank towns.

We woke up the next morning near Rugby, North Dakota, the geographic center of North America. We enjoyed breakfast while viewing a gorgeous sunrise, contrasting with the glistening white blanket of snow across the vast flatlands.

We whistled through Fort Peck, Montana, which features an earth-filled dam 250 feet high and four miles across the Missouri River. It was constructed in 1940. This is where we had lived six months in 1946 while Ormie worked driving a large dirt mover.

Our last night out we sat in Spokane, once again switching cars. In the morning we crossed the Cascade Mountains over

Stevens Pass, 4,061 feet high. The best way to get across this spectacular mountain is to go under it, thanks to the 7.79 mile tunnel through it. It is the longest tunnel in the western hemisphere and was completed in 1929.

It was worth the entire trip to wind around the curves on the edge of Puget Sound, finally bringing into view the downtown area of Seattle and the famous Space Needle. While we waited for our next train, Butch came to visit us because he was working in that area of Seattle. We had a good visit between trains.

Then we were off again on the *Coast Starlight*. We had our last meal in the diner between Seattle and Portland, and arrived in Eugene on New Year's Eve just ten minutes late. We had a wonderful trip, one I wouldn't have missed for the world and one I will always remember. I highly recommend a train trip across America if you really want to see the country.

In 1988, Orm quit his job when a corporation bought the retirement center. We went to work together cleaning houses for a property manager. We worked hard and even did some yard cleaning jobs, but we made good money and enjoyed it until one day we were asked to scrub down all the rooms in one house.

"I quit. It's too hard for me anymore," I said after that job was done. Orm continued for a while but we finally decided we wanted to travel again. We still hadn't satisfied our wanderlust. Once more we sold out to hit the road. We loaded up our used 27-foot Holiday trailer, and in September of 1988 drove out of the yard, seeking more adventures.

~CHAPTER 25~
HIGHWAY HOBOS

August 31, 1988, our rent was used up, so as planned we pulled out for our next adventure. We sold everything except what would fit into our Dodge van and our 27-foot Holiday trailer. Rolling Stone and Tagalong (our CB handles) drove out of the yard to see a few things while we still felt able to travel. We promised ourselves we would settle down again before we got too senile. Also, we hoped we wouldn't run down the road dragging our sewer hose behind us, or drive so slow we would hold up traffic, and stop before we forgot which road we were on.

I guess we are gypsies at heart because we have never stayed in one place too long. We haven't gathered much moss, but we have gathered a lifetime of memories.

We left Lane County, and God willing would be back sometime the next summer. We cruised down the highway in our van, newly painted, striped and polished, our Holiday condo following closely behind. It was our home on wheels as long as we could cut the muster.

The first thing we did was try fishing on the Santiam River in Sweet Home, Oregon—with no luck. We stopped at Marlene and Norm's for an overnight visit before we headed north. We camped in Carol and Chuck's yard for three days before we hooked on to leave Oregon.

We headed for South Dakota to visit relatives and friends before going south for the winter. We traveled the Columbia Highway to Hermiston, Oregon; Walla Walla, Washington; Lewistown, Idaho; and Missoula, Montana. We arrived in Butte, Montana, and started over the Homestake Pass toward Bozeman when it started snowing hard, so we turned around to go back to Butte and parked in the Safeway parking lot till morning. We made it to Bozeman through the snow, but our windshield wipers stopped working. On top of the weather problems and mechanical problems, I came down with the flu. We just barely got parked in Bozeman when our car battery went dead. We began to wonder if we were doing the right thing when we discovered our water pipe had sprung a leak and I had a big puddle of water in front of my bed. The last straw: the beet juice spilled all over the refrigerator! This was definitely NOT our best traveling day.

The next day was better and we rolled down the highway with the sun shining brightly and our rig working better. We stopped overnight in Miles City, Montana, and called an old friend, Abe McCantz, who drove to our camp and visited awhile. We finally arrived in Lemmon, South Dakota, at sister May's. It was a wonderful reunion with her family.

We spent several days just catching up with May and her kids, going to garage sales together, going to the lake, shopping and visiting. On my birthday, September 19, we took the whole day to go to Zeona to my old stomping grounds, stopping at the old Ruby cemetery where six of my relatives are laid to rest: Grandma Julianna, Uncle Ben, Mama, Papa, sister Rose and infant sister Adele. It was nice to see someone was taking care of the old cemetery, keeping the grass cut at least. The lilac bushes and trees had grown so much, and it's a nice peaceful place out there on the middle of the prairie.

The next stop that day was Spring Creek Farm where May and I grew up. We explored the old hill we used to slide down in the winter, "Lovers Lane," which we named when we were kids, the old rhubarb patch, which only had a few stalks of asparagus now, and the chokecherry and plum trees along the creek. I stood on the spot where the sod house used to be where I was born. We walked up to the "new house" Papa built in 1922 and walked through all the rooms, upstairs and downstairs, and then the basement. Of course this sparked many memories: sitting on the steps taking turns churning, where sister Rose lay in her coffin in the cloakroom, the rooms where we slept upstairs, the east room where Papa laid out his Long Green tobacco to dry, the little west bedroom that was originally our older sister Anna's, playing house with our dolls, and many other memories. We walked up the hill to the windmill where May had stuck her finger in a hole in the pipe and got the end of it cut off, and the old chicken house where we had our play house behind it. The pump still pumped us a drink of good water. The hog house was still there, too, where we used to play house, but it was about ready to collapse. That's where we played house because it had partitions between the pens so we could each have our own "house." The place was deserted. It now belongs to someone else, and it's sad to see the house getting in poor condition even though it still seems solid.

We stopped to see the church where we attended services and went to parochial school. It is now named an historical site by the South Dakota Historical Society and is still being used; we found hymn books imprinted with "In memory of R.F. Ruby and Adele Ruby," our parents.

Next, our memory journey took us to Spring Creek School, where I spent nine years of my life attending school as a child. The windows were gone, the old bell was gone from the belfry; and the few things left inside were mouse-eaten and weather-beaten. I found one pair of high-heeled pointed-toed shoes left by the last teacher who taught there. May and I remembered the spelling bees, singing in the morning for opening exercises, YCL meetings, recitations for programs, our teachers, fellow pupils and playing outside during recess. I remembered the happy hours in the tiny library full of books that were always available for us.

We stopped to see several empty houses, including the Breidenbach and Hathaway homes, which once belonged to our neighbors and schoolmates. Then on to Dale and Jean Simons' place, about the only ones left in the community who once lived there when we did. We had more memories there to share with each other, another nostalgic time.

We drove to the Beck School, the little one-room country school I taught two years after I got my teaching certificate in 1939. It was locked up, but I peeked in the windows; still there were the familiar photos of Washington and Lincoln and the piano I had played so much. The building had been painted recently and it looked like it might still be used for school. What a wonderful day of memories.

The next day, we picked up a couple old friends in Bison, John and Myna Tescher, and they went with us to Sorum and other places around the county to reminisce about old times. Myna went to high school in Sorum the same time May and I did, so it was "old home week." We took pictures in front of the old school and the dance hall. On across the prairie, we used the old crossing on Rabbit Creek to the go to the old Willey homestead. The house was about to fall down. Orman showed us where the rattlesnake bit him when he was twelve, the old swimming hole on Rabbit Creek and the hill they slid down in winter all the way to the creek. We stopped at the old Date store, vacated several years before, where Orman and John found some old bottles of castoria and vanilla still on the shelf in the basement.

On September 24, after a wonderful nostalgic visit on the prairie, we left Lemmon, South Dakota. We stopped at my brother Carl and Ruth's old ranch and followed them to their new home in Newell, South Dakota, where they had retired. We stopped to visit another brother, Paul, and his wife Nordis on their farm north of Sturgis, South Dakota. On the way to

Sturgis we experienced an old-fashioned electrical storm, lightning and thunder and hard rain. Now we knew we were home in South Dakota.

The next stop was Boulder Park Campground, where we raised our kids from '56 to '66. The old house and campground looked pretty much the same. My niece Hannah and her husband Allen drove us back to the subdivision we had started and up Willey Lane, where we saw that quite a few more houses had been built. Boulder Park School still stood where I saw my kids trudge down the hill to school every morning. I remembered Butch mowing the grass in the park, and the girls raking up the pine needles and pulling weeds for a penny apiece. It was a nostalgic time.

We traveled on to Deadwood, then to Spearfish, where we attended Black Hills Teachers College in 1938-39. More happy memories met us there as we recalled our college days and the times we had together when we first started to get acquainted with each other. Spearfish is where we really started our life together because it's where we fell in love.

On to Rapid City to visit relatives and friends, and this time we took the time to drive around town to find all the places we once lived. It was especially fun to see our house on Elmhurst Drive with an apartment house built on the empty lot where we had planned to build our new house one day.

We were off to Wyoming on October 3 to visit our old stomping grounds in Grand Junction, Colorado, another time for precious memories. We camped in the same campground we had lived in while we were waiting to close on our house on Thompson Road in 1974, the last place we lived before we left Grand Junction in 1976. We visited friends and enjoyed looking over the area, and one morning went to the Colorado National Monument for old time's sake. It's as beautiful as ever; God's work never changes. The same large monoliths loom up from the deep canyons, the same pinion pine and Utah junipers dot the huge rock formations.

The Colorado National Monument consists of over 20,000 acres of canyons and mesas, at an elevation of 7,107 feet at the highest point. There are sheer 300-foot cliffs from the road to the canyons below, 23 miles around the Rim Rock Drive. One monolith called Independence Rock stands in the middle of one of the canyons by itself and is a spectacular sight. It was dedicated as a national monument in the 1930s.

We visited old friends Smoky and Emma Harbour in Montrose and Rudy and Mary Volk at Somerset. We drove up the winding road to Rudy and Mary's house at 10,000 feet altitude and took pictures of the Raggedy Mountains and their old house.

It was time to move on and out of Colorado. We headed south to Four Corners where Colorado, New Mexico, Utah and Arizona all come together at a point. The monument was completed in 1961. This is the only place in the United States where you can touch four states at the same time.

We landed at Prescott, Arizona, stayed for about a week. It's a unique place and we liked it a lot. We thought maybe we might come back there to settle down someday. It has a population of 17,000, altitude 5,347 feet. Summer temperatures average 70 degrees. In 1864 the town of Prescott was formed, and Arizona became a US territory. Ft. Whipple Military Post was established and the territorial capital was Prescott. We enjoyed seeing the old homes in the area and the historic museum.

On October 22, we pulled our rig eight miles to Prescott Valley, where we parked at Peddlers Pass, a big flea market. We set up there, paid our rent for two days and set up to sell our stuff. I had been making crocheted angels, doilies and other needle crafts, and it was nearing Christmas. We cleared $69 and had my little handmade Santa Claus stolen. The next day we cleared $109, packed up and left about 2:00, headed for Bullhead City, which would be a beautiful drive over the mountains. We pulled across the bridge to Laughlin, Nevada, and parked at the Riverside Casino along with hundreds of other RVs. We gambled a little and had a chicken buffet supper for $1.79 each.

We explored the casinos and ate cheap meals for a couple days and decided to try our luck at fishing, so got licenses for both Arizona and Nevada and camped at Davis Dam on the Colorado River. By the time our five-day licenses ran out, Orm had caught five nice catfish, two pounds apiece. One day was too windy to fish so we drove over to the Regency Casinio for spareribs, $1.55 for four ribs, baked beans, garlic bread and peaches. Then we deposited $2.00 in a poker machine.

~Chapter 26~
Back to the Colorado River

On February 13 we headed for Yuma, Arizona, and camped at Senator Wash, one of the BLM camps on the desert. We found our spot near the All American Canal where we had a nice view of the canal and the mountains and it was only a short walk to go fishing. We spread our carpet on the ground in front of the trailer and stayed about a month. The name of our camp was Quail Hill; it cost only $25 a month, but about once a week we had to leave to dump the holding tank and get water. Our closest neighbor was 90-year-old Robby Robinson, a delightful old fellow. He said he had been all over the United States several times, traveling all alone for 25 years.

Our old friends from South Dakota, John and Esther Fuller, found us at Quail Hill after we had written them a Christmas card to tell them where we planned to be. We had a great visit with them for a couple days and went to Algadona, Mexico, together. We drove to the Yuma base and watched the Golden Knights parachute group jump; there were 49 men and one woman. They claim to be the best parachute team in the country. John and Ormie played golf and we all went to see the old Territorial Prison in Yuma. Every evening we played whist, an old card game we all learned as kids. It seemed like we jumped from 1946 when we all lived in the same complex at Ft. Peck, Montana, to 42 years later. We hadn't seen much of them in between.

Will and Lois caught up with us at Quail Hill, and our old friends, Frank and Hazel Kalousek, also found us there. We had good visits with both couples. I had the flu for a few days and had to go to the doctor to get cough syrup and antibiotics for bronchitis. Sister Gladys and friends Joe and Irene came to visit. We also spent time fishing out of the canal and caught a few catfish there.

On March 20 we decided to move back to Empire Landing at Parker. When we got there, we walked down to our fishing hole, but we didn't fish because of the wind. Will and Lois were already there, and we had good times together going to the flea market and eating out.

Some days it was almost 90 degrees, so we started to talk about heading north. We had been on the road for seven months. However, Jim and Mary Morgan and her folks, Fern and Tiny, showed up. It was good to see them all again so we decided to stay a little longer.

On April 3 Will and Lois Glenn pulled out to head for home. The rest of us again moved over to Crossroads Camp. But on April 9 we had survived a week of very hot weather — up as high as 107 — but we had so much fun we hated to give up. We survived the heat by hooking up two fans to our generator, then spraying ourselves and each other with water from a spray bottle (dear Mary's idea).

On April 15 we found ourselves camping alone for the first time since March 1. The weather was too warm, though, and we decided to leave Arizona. April 17 after Jim and Mary left, we took off for areas farther west, to Lancaster, California, to visit relatives before we headed north again. We stopped in Victorville to see the Roy Rogers Museum and then camped at Saddleback State Park east of Lancaster.

The next day we backed the Holiday into the backyard of Beebe and Laura's home, where we stayed for three nights, visiting them and Dolyce and Bob.

On April 25 we were off to Kernville to meet Jim and Mary at Camp 9 near Kernville. They weren't there, but we camped there for the night. They showed up later and took us on a tour of the area before they headed for Bakersfield. The next day we moved away from Lake Isabella and camped at Halfway Camp on the Kern River. We stayed in the area until May 8. Kernville is between the Sierra Mountains and the desert and has an elevation of 2,500 feet. Summers are hot and dry, with high average temperature of 95. The Tubatukabal and Kawaus Indians originally inhabited the valley, but Spanish missionaries came in the late 1700s. Permanent white settlers came for gold in 1854. They founded the settlement of Whiskey Flat, later to be known as Kernville.

The Isabel Dam was constructed in the 1940s, and by the 1950s the Kern Valley had gained its reputation as a sportsman's paradise. Isabella Lake is the largest reservoir in southern California.

We took off for Success Lake near Portersville. We caught some nice trout and stayed a couple nights just to relax and fish before we headed for Fresno to Jerry and Nancy's. Over the weekend they took us up to Yosemite National Park. The highlights of our trip were: Yosemite Falls, which drops 2,445 feet from the rim of the valley floor; Half Dome, 4,852 feet high, carved by the Ice Age glaciers; Sequoia National Park, which has the world's largest trees (and they are majestic); and Grant Grove Park, which was created in 1890 to protect the giant sequoia trees from the lumberman's axe. The General Grant tree is the third largest living tree in the world, and it's the nation's Christmas tree. The Big Stump Basin shows huge sequoia stumps, some as much as 24 feet across. The sequoia has a lifetime of 1,500 years.

On May 17 we made the trip to Sebastopol to visit Gladys and family. We went with Gladys to Ft. Bragg and Lucerne to visit friends Joe and Irene and cousin Fern. We had a great visit, and on May 24 we finally headed north to Oregon. On the way we camped along the beach right on the Pacific Ocean, and fished some, with no luck.

We met Carol and Chuck at a camp at Siltcoos Lake in

Oregon and spent a little time there fishing and visiting. Then we went to Corvallis to Marlene and Norm's and camped in the city park while we caught up with them and Eric and Ryan. From there we went north to Bonnie and Russ's, where we stayed a couple nights, then on to Washington to Butch and Katie's. While there I spent a few days in the hospital due to angina and was released with new heart medication.

June 30 was the end of ten months on the road. *It's still good if our health holds out*, I wrote in my diary. I felt better and Orm went for his checkup. We stayed in Butch's backyard at Lake Desire until September 14. We both had several stays in the VA hospital getting checked out, and I had an angiogram. We enjoyed our stay there, going to garage sales, going to town to do our laundry once a week and just relaxing. We had fun taking our grandson Jesse to some of his soccer games and visiting with Butch, Katie and our granddaughter Kristamae.

July 9 was a big day for us when we went with Butch and Katie (their treat) to the Kingdome in Seattle to watch the Mariners play the Cleveland Indians. After the game, we all went to a Mexican restaurant for supper.

Then we had a big barn sale while at Butch and Katie's. In August we watched the place and took care of all the animals while they went to Orcas Island.

On September 3, Val and Terry came from Ohio for a visit. We picked them up at the airport and had a great visit. Carol and Chuck also came that night, and the next morning we all took off for Anaccortes, where we caught the ferry to Orcas Island in the San Juans. Marlene and Norm and their boys came too, and we had 14 around our trailer. It was a beautiful reunion.

It was our first anniversary on the road, and we were more determined than ever to continue as long as our health permitted and the Lord willed. We had a wonderful year, in spite of a few problems. It was a great way to start our second year with our family all together. We missed the four who weren't there—Jennie, Todd, Terry and Heather. All good things must come to an end, and we left the beautiful island, back to Butch and Katie's yard.

On September 8 we all made a trip to Mount Rainier. Val and Terry stayed until Sept. 12. On March 2, 1889, Mt. Rainier, called Tahoma by the Indians, was made a national park by Congress. It stands 14,410 feet high.

We made plans to meet my sister May in Yakima, Washington, on October 3. We went back to Oregon and spent a week with Marlene and Norm and boys; we camped in the Corvallis City Park, driving back and forth to their house. We had some great times with them. We headed for Carol and Chuck's and then to Sunnyside, Washington, to park in Arlene's driveway while May was there. We enjoyed our visit with Arlene, her family and May. One day Wayne and Pam took us to Yakima to the fair. May and I copied some tapes Richard had made. It was a good time, but we got itchy feet and decided to head south for the winter.

On October 1 we took off to Pendleton. May, Arlene and Bub followed us. They stayed in a motel and we stayed in our trailer. The next morning we headed south, and they went back to Sunnyside. We stayed at Parma, Idaho, that night; the next night we parked behind the Say When Casino in McDermott, Nevada. We had clam chowder there for supper. We traveled through Winnemuca and Tonapah, Nevada, and from there to Death Valley, where we stayed about a week. The weather was beautiful but the temperature got past 90 a couple times.

In 1933 President Herbert Hoover proclaimed Death Valley a national monument. It has over two million acres, rich in many minerals, borax being the main product. It gets very hot in the summer; the highest temperature ever recorded was 134.

~Chapter 27~
From Death Valley Onward

We first came to Scotty's Castle and then to Furnace Creek, where the elevation is -196, one of the lowest places in the Western Hemisphere. The actual lowest spot is at Badwater in Death Valley, which is 282 feet below sea level. It is also one of the hottest points in the world, with Telescope Peak in the background rising 11,049 feet above sea level.

Scotty's Castle was named after a prospecting miner called Scott who really didn't own any part of the castle, but who hornswoggled a wealthy couple (the Johnsons) in the east to stake him and never did find gold. When the Johnsons came to check on where their money was going, they loved the climate, became healthier and finally built their home (the castle) and furnished it nicely. They gave Scotty a room even though he had swindled them for years. He told everyone it was his castle built with the gold he had found in Death Valley. He is buried on the hill behind the castle.

Leaving Death Valley, we went to Laughlin, Nevada, then to Prescott, Arizona. From there we went to Peddlers Pass, and stayed in Salome, Arizona. We arrived at Parker the next day and backed into our favorite spot at Empire Landing. Then we had the surprise of our lives. We were at the flea market in Parker on Friday for something to do, and guess who caught up with us there, none other than May and Bub.

They followed us down, and May stayed with us for about a month. We had some great times with her, and when she got ready to go home, we took her to Phoenix to catch her plane home.

On December 7 we left to go to Quartsite to take in the giant Four Corners swap meet. We planned to meet Jim and Mary at Palo Verdes and have Christmas with them for old time's sake. We stayed at Quartsite a couple nights and took off for Blythe and Palo Verdes. Jim and Mary found us parked where we met the first time we camped there the year before. We followed them to a spot on the canal where Tiny and Fern and another couple were parked. We settled in, got ready for Christmas, wrote cards and did our shopping at the Portola Date Gardens. We did a lot of fishing, visiting and enjoying the beautiful California weather. Christmas Day we set up tables outside and had a potluck dinner. We shared a wonderful meal with great company. We decorated some bushes outside the trailer with Christmas ornaments and garlands. It was quite crude, but somehow I had to make it seem like Christmas. A hunter brought us a wild goose, so I cooked it with cornbread stuffing for Christmas dinner and made my sweetie's favorite pumpkin pie and cranberry sauce.

From Palo Verdes we all pulled out to go to Finney Lake and then to the Slabs again, where we had potluck with the Glenns for New Year's Day. We then went back to Quail Hill at Yuma.

On January 22, May and her friend Leona drove over from Phoenix, where they stayed in an apartment for the winter. We went with them to Campo, California, for Leona to visit some of her relatives.

John and Esther came again to visit us at Quail Hill. We had some good whist games and went with them to San Luis, Mexico. We visited back and forth with the Tom Eggers and the Frank Kalouseks while we camped there. If we couldn't contact them on our CB we could always use pay phones somewhere in camp.

On February 22, we took off for Phoenix to visit May and Leona. We stopped at Welton to see the old car museum and stayed all night in a rest area. We dug out our violin and keyboard and had a little jam session all by ourselves, with only the truckers to bother us. We got into Phoenix the next day, found their apartment and parked behind the apartment complex.

On February 26 we got in May's car and drove with her to the Grand Canyon. We had a nice trip. We stopped on the way to see Montezuma's Castle, a five-story, 20- room dwelling built against the base of a cliff by the Simaqua Indian farmers early in the 12th century. It stands in a cliff recess 100 feet above the valley. The castle has stood for over 600 years and is one of the best preserved historic structures in the Southwest. We stayed in Flagstaff that night.

The next day we toured Grand Canyon all day, stopping on many of the rim views and seeing many spectacular views of the canyon from all angles. The last turnoff was at Desert View Watchtower, an interesting way to end the tour. The Watchtower was erected in 1932, is 70 feet high and 30 feet wide at the base. It is the highest point in the South Rim, rising 7,522 feet above sea level. We arrived back home to Phoenix that night about 9:00.

We rested a day after the trip to Grand Canyon before picking up Leona at the airport, and went to the Apache Trail in the Superstition Mountains to Tortilla Flat, a quaint little tourist trap with a restaurant and country store. We had to stop there as the road was washed out ahead. The Apache Trail is Arizona Highway 66, a magic thread that weaves its way through the mountains to wonderful fishing in the Salt River chain of lakes: Canyon, Apache and Roosevelt Lake.

Bonnie and Jack Payne came to visit one evening while we camped there. They took us out to eat and back to their house for a nice visit.

We declared March 3 moving day again. We left May and Leona and the city and headed out to Lake Pleasant, 30 miles out and camped for the night. The next night we drove off the road to Alamo Lake State Park and found a nice park, a beautiful place, but the access was not good for fishing so we just relaxed and stayed the night.

When we returned to Parker and Empire Landing we found Will and Lois camped there. We stayed in the Parker area until April 7, when we started wending our way toward Oregon with Will and Lois. First we went north of Parker to Jump Off Point on Lake Havisu to spend some time with George and Dorothy Claypool, friends we had met in Parker. We camped there and stayed three nights while the guys fished out of George and Dorothy's boat and caught a few fish. When they went home, we started north to Lake Havisu City and parked at Wal-Mart for the night. The next day we drove to Hoover Dam and parked at the Railroad Pass Casino for the night. Then it was off to Henderson, Nevada, the next day and we camped at Las Vegas Wash Camp, a real nice camp where we would stay awhile. Orm caught a few stripers and I just relaxed.

One evening we went in to Henderson and had dinner with Will and Lois's friends, Joe and Alma, and went to their house afterwards. Orm had to ask to use their bathroom. I could tell by the look on his face he was in trouble. He had eaten too much salad, and I knew he couldn't tolerate it. I cringed as the odor wafted out of their bathroom.

"It's kind of a family trait; he has trouble when he eats too much salad. We call it the Willey curse," I explained because we had never met these people before.

"You mean the whole family is full of shit?" Joe said, and the ice was broken.

Las Vegas Wash, where we camped for a week, was first used in 1829 by Joe Antoni Armijo, who was traveling from New Mexico to Los Angeles. Today the trail is known as the Old Spanish Trail. Hoover Dam was completed in 1935 when Lake Mead began to form. The lake is 115 miles long, has over 550 miles of shoreline, is over 585 feet deep and can store 28,537,000 acre feet of water. Lake Mead's primary function is water storage and power generation, but has become a major recreation area.

April 19 was moving day again, and we went on to Tonapah, where we stayed at the rest area north of there. We drove on to Fallon the next day, where we hunted for a tire for the trailer. The day after that we drove in the rain to Sparks and parked in the Nugget RV parking lot. In Susanville the next day we had our tire mounted, then continued to Goose Lake State Park just over the line in Oregon.

We headed for LaPine, where we got new tires for the "condo" and stayed all night next to a restaurant there. The next day we made it to Oakridge, stayed all night, continued on to Pleasant Hill and ate at a drive-in. We decided to say goodbye to the Glenns and head southward. We turned our wheels south to Roseburg, where we have been most of the time since. After two good years of traveling and camping, we made the decision to settle down again.

We parked our rig in the park at the fairgrounds and started looking for housing. We bought our home in Winston, Oregon. We waited for the house to be built and made several trips to Washington, for the Willey reunion in July and to help Butch and Katie get ready for the reunion. Relatives came from California, Ohio and Oregon, and the RVs all parked in the yard above the barn. We had a baseball game, horseshoe and other games. We had a big salmon barbecue one night and Butch announced the little program and meeting. He explained Kristamae's health situation, and several people put money in a donation can they put out.

Soon after the reunion ended we came back to check on the house often and stayed at the Safari Campground. On October 19, 1990, we moved out of the trailer and into the new house. Time to settle down—we'd "been there and done that," we told ourselves. We would be "at home" again with a yard and a three-bedroom house on Galaxy Drive.

~CHAPTER 28~
AT HOME IN WINSTON

We got traveling off our mind for a while and our new house was ready to move into, so on October 19, 1990, we unloaded the Holiday and moved everything we owned into our house at 405 NW Galazy Drive in Winston, Oregon. Marlene drove down from Corvallis and helped us move. We could hardly believe how much stuff we had when we unloaded. We now had three big closets plus an entrance closet, and it took almost all of that closet space to hold it all. We put our camping dishes into the cupboards and took the mattresses out of the trailer to use in our new bedroom until we could find a bed. We had so much fun settling into a house again, but were not sorry we had two full years on the road doing what we wanted to, touring the western United States. We enjoyed spending the winters in southern California and Arizona and the summers in the Northwest.

To find furniture, we went to a lot of garage sales. We practically furnished our house that way, including a refrigerator, washer and dryer. They all continued working as long as we lived in Winston. We decided we deserved good easy chairs and went to Sears to purchase a recliner for each of us. Our Catnappers did the job so much better than our tiny easy chairs we had in the trailer. We had almost forgotten what a recliner felt like.

Orm started doing the yard work and I began keeping

house again and we both loved it. Orm went to the VA golf course quite often when he got bored, and soon he had a volunteer job there manning the golf shack four hours once a week. That entitled him to play golf whenever he wanted, which worked out well for him.

For years my hobby has been needlework—crochet, knitting, tatting and plastic canvas. In the evenings I picked up my needles and worked on something, either for Christmas gifts or something for myself. One night I picked up a ball of crochet thread off the end table beside my chair; there was a crochet hook sticking out of it, and I decided to make a doily. But I would need a pattern. Just for the fun of it, I decided to see if I could make one without a pattern. A couple hours later, I spread out my work on the carpet; I looked at it closely and decided it was quite pretty. All these years I had been using someone else's patterns but I always wished I could make my own. I had admired patterns in magazines and wished I had that kind of talent.

I had nothing to lose so I typed up the instructions for my doily, wrote a cover letter and sent it to the *Workbasket* magazine, which I had been subscribing to for years. About a week later the editor, Roma Jean Rice, called. I'll never forget her name because she was the one who helped me launch a new career after the age of 70.

She said, "We would like to publish your doily. How much do you want for it?"

"I have no idea how much you pay for these things," I answered as I almost swallowed my tongue. "Would you care to make me an offer?"

"We pay anywhere from $50 to $250 depending on the size and design. Would you accept $85 for this small doily?" she asked.

"Of course, thank you very much," I quickly answered. In about a month my first check arrived, and I couldn't believe my eyes. That was the beginning of a twelve-year career in

Em's Needlecraft Designs. I am still designing some yarn projects even though my vision has deteriorated due to macular degeneration. To date, 170 of my designs have been published in about 35 magazines, ten books and several pamphlets containing my designs exclusively. It has been so much fun and given me something to look forward to in my aging years. My only regret is that I didn't start designing and marketing my needlecraft many years ago.

Our life in Winston included almost weekly trips to the senior center for lunch, where we met our new friends—Hugh and Bobbie Miller, Jim and Chris Risley and John and Leola Cole. We learned how to play Pinochle with all three couples and drew names at Christmas and gathered together for potlucks and exchange of gifts. Those were good times we treasured and we still love to play the game. However, two members of our group have passed on, so we miss the group we used to play Pinochle with.

When I first met Leola Cole, I knew she had Parkinson's Disease. But when you have a friend like Leola, you forget about her disease and just enjoy being with her. A brave soul, she carried on her life as normally as possible. She always had a smile and encouraging words for everyone. She had a deep love for the Lord that showed in her everyday actions, but she never tried to push off her beliefs on others. She taught by her own example. I could talk to Leola about anything and I knew it would stay with her. We had many heartwarming conversations about life. Not a day passed without a telephone visit with her. Finally, in 1998, she had a stroke, which took her to the hospital and finally to her reward. She suffered a lot, but never made life miserable for others because of the disease. I miss her, my best friend Leola.

In the ten years we lived in Winston I stayed involved in my needlecrafting career, but we hadn't had quite enough of the outdoors and fishing. We took the little 17-foot trailer out on weekends to go fishing at some of our favorite spots in western Oregon—Lemola Lake east of Roseburg, Fall Creek Reservoir east of Eugene, and the Rogue River at Gold Beach, Oregon. After a couple years with the "little shit" (my name for the little trailer) we no longer wanted to bother with hooking up the trailer, so we sold it and looked for a small motor home. My niece Carol and her husband Chuck helped us find a 23-foot Winnebago. We enjoyed lots of fishing trips to Lemola Lake, Rogue River, and other places with Carol and Chuck, Leonard and Jackie Woods and John and Leola. Our last trip was to Gold Beach with our friends John and Leola, our good fishing buddies. We kept the Winnebago until we moved from Winston.

I think the most favorite event in the 1990s was the celebration of Ormie's and my 50th wedding anniversary. Our daughters Valerie and Marlene arranged the big party for us on the beach at Gearhart by the Sea in Gearhart, Oregon. Sixty relatives and friends came from all over Oregon, Washington, California, Wyoming and South Dakota. Orman and I each had sisters who attended: Bonnie Steeves, Gladys Jackson, and May Hathaway. My brother Paul Ruby also attended. Our daughter Valerie, her husband Terry and son Todd, and our daughter Marlene and her son Ryan represented our immediate family. In addition, six nephews and six nieces came with spouses and children. To fill out the group were eight couples who are all old friends. Over 100 anniversary cards were received at the party, most sent to the girls ahead of time.

Val and Marlene started the program by pinning flowers on both of us. Then they asked anyone who wished to to get up and say a few words. Chuck Breidenbach got up and told how Ormie took him fishing and how we taught him to play poker. He added that he's still losing to us too. Boyd Ruby told how we sold his RV storage place for him. Frank Kalousek got up and talked about going to grade school with me and then meeting Orman when they were in the National Guard together.

When people got through talking, the girls put on a tape and asked Ormie and me to lead the waltz. We did and a lot of people joined us to dance. Then Lois Zilko, Lois Glenn and our grandson Ryan read poems that had been written about us, and one I had written for our fortieth anniversary. It was time to cut the cake my niece Carol had made for the occasion. It was a tall three-tiered cake decorated with red roses. But first our grandson Todd made a toast to us. I wish I had a copy of it.

After the cake was served, everyone dispersed until the evening, when we all gathered again to have dinner, a joyous occasion for us. My nephew Wayne Ruby read a brochure my sister May had made up for us for our 50th. Following is an excerpt from "Affections and Memories":

A Pair of Sweethearts

God knew you both and that is why
He chose you from the start
T o share as one, to be as one — One life, one love, one heart.

From May (sister of Em)

~Chapter 29~
More Winston Memories

We enjoyed our home on the corner of Lookingglass Road and Galaxy Drive. Ormie loved hiking up to the top of our hill where he could see the Bears' Den at the Wildlife Safari. He kept our yard mowed, and the first few years we lived there I set out petunias, Shasta daisies, azalea and other flowers; we also had a couple tomato plants.

But it wasn't long until Ormie got a little bored and decided to look for a job. He was 75 when he took off one morning to find work. He came home that afternoon and announced, "I go to work Monday at K-Mart as a greeter." He worked there quite awhile, until his three-day-a-week job turned into seven days. That didn't leave us time to go camping and fishing, so he resigned. That was his last paying job, but he volunteered at the VA golf course for four hours once a week, which entitled him to play golf free anytime he chose.

In 1997 we threw a surprise 80th birthday party for Orman. He knew our immediate family would be there, but the surprise was when his sister Gladys, her son Max, and her daughter Bonnie walked in. They had driven from Sebastopol, California, for the occasion, as had his nephew and his wife, Jerry and Nancy, who also drove from Fresno, California. All my nieces and their husbands arrived at the party, along with two of Orm's army buddies from World War

II, Frank Kalousek and Lyle Becker. We had dinner catered at a local restaurant. Most of the guests came to our house afterward to visit and have a buffet supper, a fun time for everyone.

We had been in Winston a couple years when we met our good friends Jackie and Leonard Woods, who lived down the street from us. Orm and Len met on the riverbank fishing. They became good fishing buddies and went deer hunting several times; and they brought home game. Jackie and Leonard are loyal friends to this day, even though Leonard and Orman have both given up fishing and hunting.

Through the ten years we lived in Winston, we had lots of visitors from both our families and from friends as well. We went to Carol and Chuck's place in Tualatin often, where we saw my brother Fred and his wife Naomi whenever we made the trip. We also made numerous trips to Hillsboro to see Orm's sister Bonnie, and moved her several times until she finally ended up in the nursing home there.

I carried on with my needlecraft business, but in 1997 my right eye went bad with macular degeneration. I couldn't see well to type up my craft instructions, so I bought a word processor thinking that would help. However, after bringing it home, I found I couldn't even read the operating instructions, so we took it back to the store. The only answer for me then was a computer. I had to eat the words I had spoken earlier: "I'm never going to have one of those things." And my husband didn't encourage me to get one either.

One day Ormie came home from his volunteer job at the golf course and said to me, "There's a guy at the golf shack who wants to sell his golf cart. He doesn't want too much for it and I'd like to buy it. What do you think, honey?"

I jumped at the chance. "I think you should buy it, dear, and then I can have my computer," I said. He agreed and we both had a new toy to play with. Val and Terry came down, helped me pick out my first computer, and set it up for me. They gave a few lessons, and I soon learned to use the word processor. Eventually I got e-mail, and that is a big pleasure for both of us, allowing us to hear from our family almost daily, and friends often, too. Orm still uses his golf cart as often as weather allows and I use my computer every day.

The most important event in 1999 was the arrival of our blessing, our first great-granddaughter, Emma Corrine Stubbe. She was born on January 25. I was almost 79 and Orm almost 82. We didn't get to meet her till she was nine months old, but it was well worth the wait. She is a beautiful child with a sweet personality whom no one can resist. Little Emma is a doll.

We aged a little in the ten years we lived in Winston. Orm still had his equilibrium problem, and after rolling down the hill a few times while mowing or weed eating he decided he had enough of yard work. My vision gradually worsened and I wondered if my cooking was clean anymore. When I reached up in the cupboard for a glass one day that stuck to the cupboard, I knew I wasn't getting my dishes clean either. We had to do something different, so we started looking around for a different place to live. Two new assisted living places were under construction in Roseburg, just seven miles from Winston. We went to look at both of them and made the decision to move.

I roasted my "last" turkey that Thanksgiving for my family and my daughters, Valerie and Marlene, brought the rest of the meal. We invited Leola and John to join us, and it was fun doing this one last time, with the girls' help, of course. However, I realized it was too much work for me. The decision was made; we would move to a new assisted living place. We thought long and hard about it, and weighed the pros and cons.

"Now we know everything won't be perfect in the new place," Orman kept warning me. But we thought we had to do it.

We had a lot of work to do. First we advertised the motor

home because it had sat in the driveway a whole year. Several people came to look at it, and finally the right person came with cash in his hand. We had many fun fishing trips with it, and now we saw our plaything back out of the driveway for the last time. That was the first hurdle.

We started sorting through things in the house and garage, and Marlene came down and helped us hold a big garage sale one Saturday. As she sold things, I kept moving more items out to the garage. People came in the house to look at the furniture we decided to sell, and when my curio cupboard walked out the door, it gave me a lump in my throat. I sold everything out of it except the dishes my girls wanted. We kept on going through things, and planned to have a final garage sale as soon as the house sold.

We then put our home on the market. The realtor put the sign up on the front lawn on a Saturday, and the following Monday it sold, so we felt like it was meant to be. We agreed to give possession on January 1, 2000.

Now we really had to get to work. We looked at both assisted living facilities in Roseburg and put down some money on Callahan Village. But when our house sold right away, we chose to move to McAuley House because it was ready to receive residents, while Callahan wasn't quite ready to open.

We carried more things to the garage for our final sale, but then we both got the flu and I ended up in the hospital. Our wonderful kids, Marlene, Valerie and Terry, came and moved us. I was still in the hospital on moving day and didn't get to help. Orm didn't help much either because he also had the flu. Our plan to move ourselves "while we're still able to do it ourselves" didn't happen.

~Chapter 30~
One More Mountain to Climb

Our family worked hard getting us moved into our new place. They had most everything moved and planned to have our final garage sale their last day in town. But lying in the hospital, I told Val and Marlene, "There's no way I'm going to let you have a garage sale." I wanted to spend a little time with my daughters before they had to leave for their own homes. Louise's Second Hand Store had told me earlier she would take everything on consignment. She sent her crew to pick up everything — right down to the last can full of garbage. Under the circumstances, it was a great deal. The house was cleaned out and ready for possession. Val, Terry and Marlene finished moving the rest of our things to McAuley House, where we had decided to live. Orman moved in without me because I spent a few more days in the hospital. When I got out, I had only a few boxes left to unpack because the girls had put most everything away for me. We adjusted quickly to our new way of life, and for a while, things went smoothly for us.

There are advantages to this style of assisted living, and also a few disadvantages if you happen to choose the wrong place. We had security; at 8:00 p.m. every night the doors were locked so no outsiders could get in. While Orman went to play golf or to do his volunteer job at the VA golf course, I had only to pull a string inside the apartment to get medical help if needed. One day I had chest pains, and when the second nitroglycerin pill didn't take away the pain, I pulled the string. Within a few minutes three people came, took my blood pressure and pulse and stayed with me until the third nitro took away the pain. I felt lucky to have someone there helping me.

At McAuley House they served three meals a day, with two choices of menu for lunch and dinner and a variety of breakfast choices every morning. Not only did someone else cook, they did the dishes and cleaned up the mess too. Someone picked up our garbage every morning and made our beds. Every Thursday someone picked up our laundry.

"Your apartment will be cleaned every week," they said. Every Friday Loretta the housekeeper came in to vacuum, mop the bathroom and put clean linens on our beds. That was the best service we had at the facility.

"We don't iron," they said, and we didn't expect them to, but it would have been nice to have our shirts and pants hung on hangers when they came out of the dryer. So we began to do our own outer clothing and let them do the linens and underwear. One day the caregiver brought our laundry back with our towels and bed linens missing. They finally found them in someone else's apartment.

"Your beds will be made every morning," the administrator said, but they were rarely touched until after 10:00 a.m. and sometimes not at all. We decided to make the beds ourselves.

They said we would have a nurse on duty, but she was there only three days a week. We had mail delivery to a private mailbox in the facility. We had planned activities through the week including spelling contests, Bingo, music, trips to various places and bus transportation for doctor appointments and shopping. The beauty shop at McAuley House had reasonable prices and served both men and women, so we didn't have to go out for that service. We parked our car in a lighted parking lot out front. The people who worked there were caring people and treated us with respect at all times.

After living at McAuley House for a year, we became a little depressed because so many people who moved in had dementia or Alzheimer's. So we decided to look for another place to live. We wanted more alert neighbors with whom we could visit and enjoy a game of cards. We tried to change what we didn't like and tried hard to accept what we couldn't change, but finally felt our mental health challenged. We had to keep our doors locked or someone might wander in and take things. One man took clothing out of the dryers when we did our laundry. To have an intelligent conversation with some of the residents was out of the question. We felt the place had become a nursing home without nurses, and we felt sorry for those residents because they didn't get the care they needed.

One weekend when Val and Terry came to visit, we all stopped at Callahan Village to check it out. It had a special and separate Alzheimer's unit where residents could get the help they needed. They had a vacancy, and once more our children insisted on moving us to a place where we could be happy.

After we had moved into the first facility, I asked at the activity meeting one day, "Anyone here like to play Scrabble?"

"I do!" said Mildred, and we made a date to play the next day in the living room. Since Scrabble is favorite game of mine, I was excited about finding someone to play with me. Within a short time into our game, it was obvious this lady didn't have the foggiest idea how to play Scrabble. She tried to make words from bottom to top and from right to left and didn't understand that each word had to connect to another one on the board. So exhausted by the time all the tiles were played by trying to teach her the game, I went home and never challenged her to another game.

"Can I help you?" I asked a bewildered lady I encountered in the hallway on the way to my apartment one day.

"Yeah, where's the bathroom?" she said. I pointed her in the right direction.

"If I had a brain I'd actually be dangerous," she whispered in my ear as she sidled up to me. I didn't know whether to laugh or cry.

One day when I decided to go downstairs on the elevator, the door opened and a lady came barreling out like she was going to a fire and almost ran over me with her wheelchair. The same day someone in an electric cart barely missed running over my toes getting into the elevator. I soon learned to keep my distance when I saw a wheelchair coming toward me.

When I got off the elevator one day I started for my room and met a feeble old lady who hadn't the slightest idea where she lived. I tried to guide her to her apartment, but she didn't even know her room number. I took her down to the office to ask the manager. It turned out she was looking for her room on the wrong floor.

One night after supper I was sitting in my recliner reading the evening paper when the door burst open and two people I had never seen before walked in without knocking and asked to see the manager.

"You'll have to take the elevator down to the first floor where the office is," I said and started leading them down the hallway toward the elevator.

"I've never used an elevator before," the lady said.

"Get in, and when the door opens, get out and you will see the office there and someone will help you," I explained as I opened the elevator door. Quickly I pushed the number 1 button and left them looking bewildered.

One of the aides did our laundry one day and had to fight off one resident who tried to steal our clothes out of the dryer. I think he got away with one of my nightgowns because I never found it after we moved.

A couple sat at the next table from us in the dining room. They shouted at each other constantly because neither one could hear a darn thing. One night at dinner they discussed their bathroom arrangements and we overheard part of the conversation.

"Well, what if my bowels break loose?" she said.

"Just let 'em go!" he answered.

Bob and Louise, both nearing 90, came to the dining room every day, each pushing a walker. They politely ignored everyone else, but talked constantly to each other. I thought they were a married couple. Not so, we found out.

"We need help in here! Bob fell out of bed!" Louise yelled as she stuck her head out of her apartment. Not long after that they asked the activity director to take them to the courthouse.

"Why do you have to go to the courthouse?" Wendy inquired.

"We have to go get our marriage license," Louise said emphatically. We later attended the wedding in the Fireside Room.

We had some good laughs at the expense of our fellow residents in both places, and I imagine some of them laughed at us, too. That's okay. We all have our own funny ways and habits developed over the many years we have lived. At times it's actually sad, but we concluded we have to have a good sense of humor if we are to live with other elderly people.

At the families' requests, several funerals were held there because some of the elderly people had only their friends at Callahan left. We never knew what might happen next in this unpredictable place. I really didn't like the idea of turning our dining room into a funeral parlor.

A lot of bright people also lived at Callahan Village with whom we could communicate, play games, and join in other activities. It was a place where interesting activities happened every day. We didn't have time to get depressed and we liked living there. We enjoyed the bright-eyed 80- and 90-year-olds who lived there.

In 2000 I celebrated my 80th birthday. Knowing how much I love the beach, my three kids and their spouses planned a wonderful party at the beach at Seaside, Oregon. They rented a big house for three days, room for all of us to sleep. They planned all the food for the weekend, complete with birthday cake and gifts. We had good visits, some poker games and lots of walks on the beach together. Todd and Liz came from Ohio, Eric from Atlanta, Georgia and Ryan from San Jose, California. The other three grandkids couldn't come.

After living at Callahan Village for two years, circumstances beyond our control forced us to move one more time. We didn't like leaving our friends there, but it resulted in a good thing for us.

We applied for VA pensions and were told we would both get one. We looked for places to live and most of them had waiting lists. Finally we found an empty apartment at Linus Oakes Retirement Center, which was expensive but it seemed the best solution for us at the time.

The Year 2000

~Chapter 31~
The Other Side of the Mountain

Butch and Jesse came down with their plumbing pickup and moved all of our stuff out of Callahan Village to Linus Oakes. We liked our new independent style of living and got more assistance than we did in the other two places. We thought it a wonderful place to live out our remaining years and were happier than we had been since we sold our home in Winston three years earlier. The people who live at Linus Oakes are one big happy family.

They served only the evening meal at Linus Oakes, and it's the best food we had eaten in three years. We had so many choices of food, and a menu that surpassed any restaurant in town. Every evening we spiffed up a little and showed up at the dining room, which was nicely decorated with tablecloths and fresh flowers on every table. Once a week they served wine for the residents and their guests. We enjoyed dinner every night complete with waiters or waitresses. However, we did enjoy fixing our own breakfasts again. We made new friends and found people to play cards with. We joined the fitness class that met three times a week and enjoyed associating with a new group of people.

We enjoyed Linus Oakes for five months, but then we started to worry. We decided this wasn't meant to be. We had applied for increased pensions but neither had come through, and one morning I said to Orm, "I know we were born to move. We are paying an awful lot for a fancy dinner every night and don't have many funds left at the end of the month to do other things we enjoy."

"Yes, I know," he said. Once again we started looking for a more suitable place to live. This time we moved to a two-bedroom, two-bath apartment that cost us less than a third as much as Linus Oakes and would give us a fully independent lifestyle again. However, we would have to do our own cooking and cleaning once again.

Marlene and Norm came and moved everything for us from Linus Oakes to Oakridge Apartments. We had one more adjustment to make in our elderly years, but we had a ground-floor apartment that was furnished with a washer and dryer, refrigerator, stove, dishwasher and garbage disposal. We were happy to be independent again. In case of an emergency, we were both able to call 911. Orman could still drive our car, so we could get to doctors' appointments and shop for groceries.

We have had variety in our lives if nothing else, and we always better ourselves every time we move. Sometimes I wonder if there are places to move to in heaven.

Several years ago when we lived in Junction City, Oregon, our friend Carl, who was legally blind, used to say, "I know I'm over the hill, but I'm having fun going down the other side." He would call us and say, "If you got the wheels, I got the dough." And then we went to the best restaurants in town. We learned a lot from Carl about growing old gracefully. He always had a smile and a positive attitude even when we knew he experienced pain. Now we are the elderly ones and I hope we can set the same example our friend did for us.

Before I end this account of our life together, I will say a few things about our families. First, my parents left us in 1954 and '55, survived by eleven of their children. We started out as twelve brothers and sisters, and only Rose preceded them in death. Then we lost Chris, and through the years Richard, Anna, Frank, Carl, Ruth and Paul. Then only May and I, the two youngest, survived. In June 2005, May left too, so I am the only surviving sibling of twelve. May and I remained close all these years, and when the others left we had each other, but now I am one, and there is no way except to conclude it must be my turn to find them all in that beautiful place someday.

Orman's dad Dode passed away in 1959. His mother Clara lived to the age of 94 and passed away in 1985. He lost his oldest brother RC during World War II, his brother Aldy in 1973 and his brother Noble in 1985. His sister Bonnie passed away in 1998. So Orman's sister Gladys and he are the only survivors in their family. But the great-grandchildren keep coming to carry on the family.

Losing family members and many friends along the way is the price we pay for living so long. We wonder why some have to leave and some stay longer. It's not for us to question because I believe God has a plan for all of us.

As I come to the end of this tale, it's fun to see what we caused when we said "I do" 62 years ago. We welcomed another great-granddaughter into our family on May 28, 2003. She is Olivia Grace Whitten, daughter of our granddaughter Jennie and her husband Al.

Elliot Eric Johnson joined our family on Mother's Day of 2004. He is the son of our grandson Eric and his wife Amy. So now there are 20, counting all in-laws and spouses. We love them all and are proud of each one.

Now in my 80s, I have taken up writing because I can see the words I write on the computer using my large-print software. My first book, *Prairie Rattlers, Long Johns and Chokecherry Wine: Memoirs of the Silent Prairie* was published by PublishAmerica and released in September 2003. It's the story of my childhood growing up in South Dakota. I use most of my time writing, and Ormie spends a lot of time on the golf course. As Carl said long ago, "We are having fun going down the other side." We will be here until the good Lord decides our time is up.

After living more than 85 years, it's hard to believe we have a difficult time making the right decisions. But in spite of some wrong decisions, we have enjoyed some of them—decisions that have taken us down roads we never planned on.

As this last chapter of *Beyond the Silent Prairie* winds down and I look back at it, I think I should write a book titled *How to Move*. My intention here is not to bring up anything from the past that would hurt anyone. I believe we have to look ahead to the future with optimism and good feelings toward each other. I also believe that forgiveness is the road to happiness. Nobody will ever be perfect, not even me.

Recently I joined a training program for the blind at American Lakes Veteran Hospital in Tacoma, Washington. I checked in for six weeks, and when I finished with the training I took home a new Gateway computer, monitor and HP printer, all with capability of large print. I am so grateful for this opportunity because it allows me to keep on with my writing.

To the readers of this book, take some advice from an old woman who has weathered lots of moves and who has enjoyed variety in life with a husband who still likes to have fun after sixty-two years of marriage:

- Live as long as you can as much as you can.
- Associate with people you like to be with.
- Make the most of each day.
- Find something to laugh about every day.
- Remember—life isn't always fair.
- Sometimes bad things happen, but life goes on.
- Be tolerant of others and respect their rights to their own beliefs and values.
- Forgiveness is the road to happiness.
- Let your goals leave a legacy for your descendants.

- Keep love in your heart.
- Above all, believe in your God, whoever He is, with all your heart.

THE END

Printed in the United States
58079LVS00002B/223-231